Praise for the first edition

"*A Time Outworn* is a first novel, a delicate, sensitive melancholy one written in a cool and lovely prose ..."
Orville Prescott, *New York Times*

"Character is very exactly caught ... and one of the most potent presences is Ireland herself, potent, volatile ... "
Jacky Gillott, *The Times*

"The prose is the sort that only a woman of genius can write, with every word like a dart at a target."
Frank O'Connor, *Harper's Bazaar*

"... Writes well, and should be listened to, even if a shade too sure of what she has to say."
Kate O' Brien, *The Irish Press*

"Her style is hard and perfect, and she has given us a considerable achievement to reckon with."
Benedict Kiely

"Congratulations are in order in the case of Miss Val Mulkerns, a young Dublin girl whose *A Time Outworn* is a sensitive, intelligent first novel."

RG, *The Irish Times*

By the same author

A Peacock Cry
Antiquities
An Idle Woman
The Summerhouse
A Friend of Don Juan
Very Like A Whale
Memory and Desire
Friends With The Enemy

A TIME OUTWORN

ANNIVERSARY EDITION

VAL MULKERNS

451
Editions

A Time Outworn
Anniversary Edition, 2025
Published by 451 Editions
Dublin
www.451Editions.com

© Val Mulkerns 1951 and 2025

ISBN: 978-1-9162975-1-7

This book is sold subject to the condition that it shall not, by way of trade or otherwise, be lent, resold, hired out, digitally reproduced or otherwise circulated without the publisher's prior consent in any form of binding, cover or digital format other than that in which it is published and without a similar condition being imposed on the subsequent purchaser.

The characters and events portrayed in this book are fictitious. Any similarity to real persons, living or dead, is coincidental and not intended by the author.

Special Note,
Anniversary Edition, 2024:

This book has been reproduced precisely from the original first edition, without updates or adjustments to the original text. It is re-published as it was published in 1951.

Printed in Ireland by Sprint Books

For 'JJ,' my father,
and to the memory of
my mother

note

Because we in Ireland (despite the
familiar charge) dramatise ourselves
as to encouraging other people to do it
for us, it is doubly necessary to state that all
the characters in this story are imaginary.

Table of Contents

Foreword – Carlo Gébler	9
Introduction – Maev Kennedy	16
Part One 　　The Last Summer	25
Part Two 　　Half in Dream	93
Part Three 　　The Third Death	185
Epilogue	237
About The Author	240

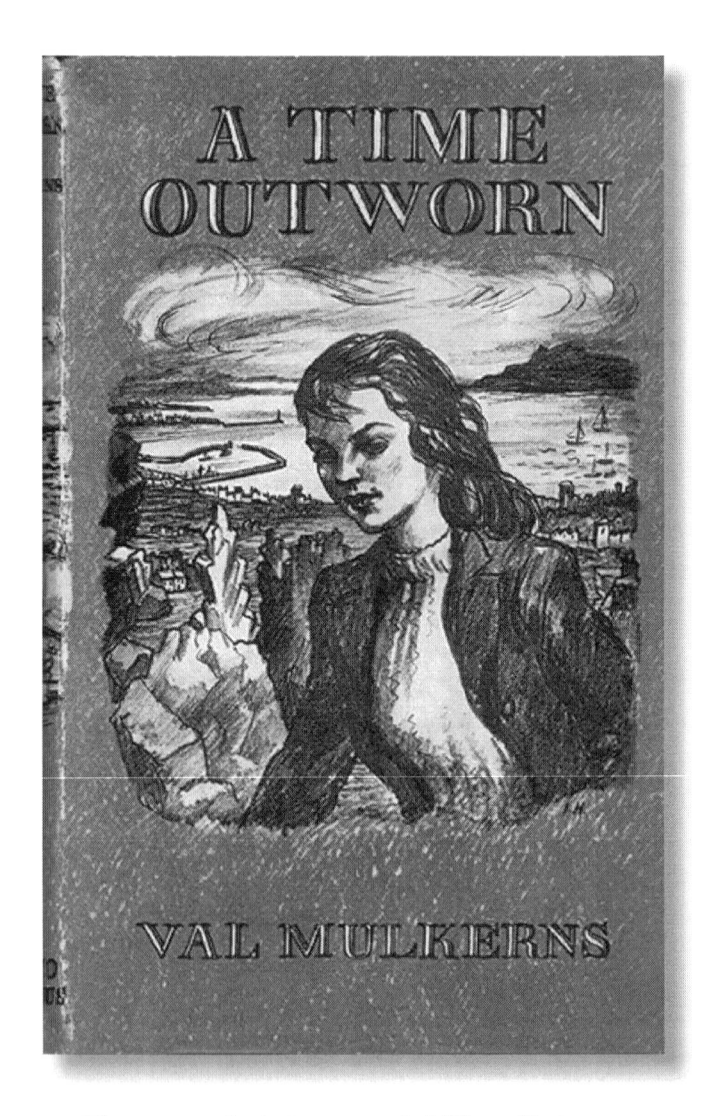

The original 1951 cover of *A Time Outworn*

Foreword

My parents were the writers Edna O'Brien and Ernest Gébler, and I spent the first two years of my life in an atmospheric house overlooking Lough Dan high in the Wicklow Hills. Just before Christmas 1955, it was sold and we moved to 29, Garville Avenue, Rathgar, Dublin. One of the reasons they bought the house on Garville Avenue was that they had close friends there, the novelist Val Mulkerns (1925–2018) and her husband, Maurice Kennedy (1924–1992), a civil servant and short story writer who moonlighted as a theatre critic on Radio Éireann. Their daughter, Maev, was my friend and playmate. Indeed, I can't remember playing with any other child during this period.

The Kennedy house was number 13 with a great beech tree at the front, a survivor of the avenue of trees that had once led to the 'Big House' which had been demolished to make way for Garville Avenue. I have been told that my father so envied the Kennedy's beech, that Maurice helped him to plant one front of our own house. Number 13 was two storeys with the best rooms on the first floor reached by granite steps. At the rear there was a purpose-built apple house, with beautiful built-in slatted shelves which, like the beech, were much admired and envied by my father.

I have vague recollections of the interior of number 13: panelled doors, old plasterwork, cast-iron fireplaces, sash windows, and green-stained light. Much stronger are my memories of typewriters standing waiting, sometimes with paper on the roller, notebooks and pens lying around, of hardback books on tables and sofas with their spines bent back, newspapers with articles marked in blue and black, and the bitter smell of carbon paper and typewriter ribbon. These were sights and smells with which I was already acquainted, for both my parents, after all, were writing all the time, and it was gratifying to find the familiar echoed in our neighbours' house. It was also misleading, for as a result of the chime I formed the impression that every house in the world was a place of literary industry. Of course, that I was so misled I also now see as a gift; for it is the case that my becoming a writer owes as much to the example of Val Mulkerns and Maurice Kennedy as it does to my parents. As I am increasingly coming to understand, what made me was not school and university and that sort of thing, as I've always believed, but certain primary experiences in childhood, of which my time in 13 Garville Avenue was one.

We left Garville Avenue (by then a family of four, my brother Sasha having arrived in 1956) and moved to London in 1958. The experience of the move was traumatic – I lost my dog, I lost Greta who looked after me, I lost Maev, I lost the marvellous garden at number 13 where I played for hours, I lost everything – and it is only now (it's another late insight) that I understand the huge impact this event had on me and how it shaped my personality.

Our new house in London stood at the top of a hill opposite Cannon Hill Common. When I was out on this great, windswept, muddy space with dotted statuesque oaks, I had many strange encounters which taught me that not all human beings were nice or good. I frequently recalled the Kennedy's marvellous garden where I had played so happily and where I had had some of my earliest aesthetic experiences of beauty and the natural world, and I experienced what I now understand was something like homesickness.

In the late sixties, my parents divorced and I went off to boarding school. My father acquired a partner, and in the late seventies he sold the house and returned to Dublin where, with the help of Maureen Cusack (the wife of the actor, Cyril) he bought a beautiful house on Coliemore Road, Dalkey, known as Cnoc Aluinn. I visited occasionally with my brother, but our filial encounters were awkward. Our father suspected we were carpet baggers, sniffing about and looking for advantage. He was lonely and isolated, but at least he reconnected with his old friends Val and Maurice.

In the early nineties, following a fall, my father, alone by this stage, went into a nursing home and I was instructed to clear his house. His library was rich and thrilling and among the volumes I found was a lovely hardback edition (though sadly lacking its dust jacket) which I took back to Enniskillen where I was living by then. The book was Val Mulkerns's first novel, *A Time Outworn*, published by Chatto & Windus in 1951. It was Maurice Kennedy's own copy; his signature is in the front, in blue ink, a clear strong signature, with an emphatic M and an emphatic K. How did my father acquire Maurice Kennedy's copy? I think Val must have passed it to him during the eighties when he was trying to write what he called his 'Auto-biog'. Thus, when I was asked to write this foreword, there was *A Time Outworn* on my own shelves waiting for me.

A Time Outworn is described on the title page as 'A novel'. The text is first person, past tense. The setting is Ireland during what is called the Emergency, which is known to the rest of the world as the Second World War. The novel's narrator is Maeve Cusack, eighteen-years-old, just finished school but will not be going to college as she hasn't done well enough in her exams. Instead of further education she must now enter the world of work and forge a life. She is very well read and thoughtful. She is also an anti-philistine, and she harbours doubts about the Free State and Irish society and the Catholic Church (though she keeps these carefully under wraps – she is in a state of internal exile, though this is a term I doubt the character would recognise).

Maeve has a boyfriend, Diarmuid Barron. He is also a reader, a believer in high culture and a sceptic but, like Maeve, not an iconoclast. Maeve and Diarmuid are a perfect match, and though they are in love and would marry, they can't – they're too young. So, whilst Diarmuid goes to college, Maeve quits Dublin and goes to a town in Tipperary to work in a library. The consequences for Maeve of this move are, in one way catastrophic and in another way, enlarging and liberating. While away in Tipperary, Maeve matures and deepens and towards the end, it appears to the reader (or it did to this reader at any rate) that she has found her way, and that finally she is on the right path.

In other words, this is a *bildungsroman*, a novel dealing with one person's formative years and spiritual education – or at least that's what it looks like. But at the same time, it isn't. Yes, it is the story of how Maeve grows, but that's a feint; that is what gets us interested in the first place and keeps us reading to the end. But what the writer is actually doing, which is much more complicated, is nothing less than offering as much of Ireland and the people who lived on the island of Ireland then, as she can squeeze in within the constraints of the story. The novel has the most extraordinarily wide social, political, cultural and geographical reach; thus, we meet many different people doing many different things in many different places. Unlike many of her contemporaries, she even includes the other Ireland – Northern Ireland – in the novel, although her characterisation of the Proddy Northern Ireland Customs folk as dour unfriendly souls, does strike me as a bit harsh. But that is small spot of imperfection and the assertion stands. There are few if any equivalent Irish novels written and published in the period with the breadth of interests in all senses that are on display in *A Time Outworn*.

The novel also needs to be celebrated for the writer's technical capacity and literary burnish. It is packed with memorable sentences and exacting descriptions. Val Mulkerns has a real aptitude for specificity and a pronounced talent when it comes to the evocation of place. The handling of chronology (*A Time Outworn* spans about two years) is also done with aplomb. The same can be said – and this is a novel with about half a dozen story lines – about the numerous narrative threads that are followed. The writer's mastery of her people and their fates is absolute; we're never lost and we're never confused.

However, for me, as a reader, Val Mulkerns's greatest achievement is the reveal (or trick if you prefer) which she practices at the end, when she discloses that although it is fiction, this is not a novel, but a memoir. What we realise when this reveal is sprung (it was not to every contemporary reader's taste when *A Time Outworn* was published but it is to mine) is that what we've been reading are words written by Maeve about her life. All along she has been writing to understand her world, to understand her place in the world and to work out where she wants to go in this world. The twist at the end satisfyingly explains how the text came into being. It isn't an untethered literary invention, but springs from the concrete: more importantly, the reveal changes our sense of everything we've read up to this point and this new understanding means everything makes total sense. Yes, of course Maeve has been telling us her story, but she's been writing as part of the practice of becoming – and so everything, not only her own story, is of interest and is a subject for her. That's why she writes about so many different people and so many different places. That's why what she produces reads like a prospectus despite the thread of *bildungsroman* running through it.

I am hugely impressed with this novel but most especially with the writer's daring re-designation of the novel at the end as a memoir. Val Mulkerns was twenty-six when *A Time Outworn* was published, but already she was a writer not only aligned with old fashioned literary virtues (clarity, lucidity, evocation of place and character, for example), but also a writer who was interested in the form, with how fiction functioned, and with how writers might make their offering better by changing the terms under which it was presented. A fictionalised memoir is an excellent conceit (especially when it is slotted, as is the case here, into a larger story, as we eventually discover is the case). It is much more interesting, to my mind, than a text that simply asks us to accept that it's a fiction, created by an author ventriloquizing a character who is speaking from the ether.

Later in life, Val Mulkerns encountered the English experimental novelist and writer BS Johnson (she writes about him brilliantly in her memoir, *Friends with the Enemy*, 2017). She understood Johnson and she was excited by what he was doing in his fiction, which sought to advance how novels might present themselves, but this should come as no surprise, I think. Though she was never as out there as Johnson was, Val Mulkerns understood the need for writers to develop the novel and the strategies underpinning their fiction, and she was no slouch herself, as her beautiful first 'novel' clearly demonstrates, when it came to developing and advancing the form.

Carlo Gébler
Tuesday 24 September 2024

Introduction

"Go on, idiot! Imagine a bookless night, a bookless tomorrow, a bookless Sunday!"

(Friday, 10 December 1943, urging herself out into a rainy night to visit the library)

On Saturday September 29, 1945 a young Dublin woman went round to the *Irish Independent* offices in Middle Abbey Street, to leave in a small ad.

"Written out it looks a bit half witted," she recorded in her meticulous diary, 'Civil Servant, 21, desires change to full-time literary work on magazine or newspaper. Has contributed to Irish periodicals.' Am doubtful now whether I want anything to come of it or not. Am ashamed to admit that more money is the only thing that would finally decide me. Leaving D'Olier House is going to be a wrench."

The diaries Val Mulkerns kept at least since the age of 10 trace the unshakable determination of a painfully earnest young woman to become a published author. From childhood she listed and commented on all the books she read, the plays, concerts (often several in a week) and occasional films she attended, in journals kept in pocket diaries, school copy books, and for two years in rough notebooks clearly liberated from the civil service stationery cupboard.

In 1943, her beloved mother Esther dead, her Leaving Cert passed but without any chance of the scholarship that would get her to university, she wrote: "am now fed up to the teeth of housekeeping" for her father and two younger brothers. When she wrote the ad (actually only 20, having rounded up her age to seem more grown up) she had achieved that great Irish aspiration, the good job in the Civil Service, and she was desperate to be rid of it.

The writer's Ireland was small and intimate in the 1940s, not to say claustrophobic. On holidays at Raphoe in Donegal in June 1946 – "that lovely enchanted interlude" she attracted the interest of three young men, kissed at least two of them in the moonlight, and dressed for dinner at the hotel, "something I've always longed to do", where she struck up a conversation with a fellow guest.

"No salt on our table, so we borrowed a salt cellar from a tall man in brown with a white, leonine head and a voice coming pleasantly from somewhere far down. He with his party was at the next table. He proved to be M. J. McManus of the Press… dear MJ, was ever man so charming? We became friends in record time," she wrote. MJ was then the first ever literary editor of the Irish Press, journalist, poet, and a humourist gently mocked by James Joyce in Finnegans Wake. Two months later she was cast into despair covering many pages when he rejected an article. Hoping for advice, she met him on August 20, 1946 at the Pearl Bar, a famous literary and newspaper hangout, opposite the back door of the Irish Times. "Dylan Thomas, all curls, with his wife and Mr Smillie were at the next table, and presently Francis McManus came in and joined us." Unfortunately she didn't record one word of the exchanges between

The diaries, 1944-47

the poet and the *Irish Times* editor, but McManus, poet and historical novelist, stayed on when the others scattered, "insisted on getting me another sherry, and said amusing things with his brilliant little eyes. He's an intelligent if spasmodic talker." There was typically Dublin gossip of the poets Austin Clarke and Seamus O'Sullivan, and the artist Sean O'Sullivan. "Learned that Seamus O'Sullivan is a soak, likewise Sean O'Sullivan. Seamus has some secret method of sobering up which is the envy of everybody, but which only takes effect in his home. When he invites you out to dinner you invariably carry him home. I gather that Austin Clarke had a spell in Venice with an ex-mistress of D H Lawrence, of which fact he is very proud."

She was also attending lectures on journalism – one by the novelist Benedict Keily, misspelled in her diary as Kylie, who would later become very important in her life. She was also part of a chain smoking writer's group meeting around a green table in Jury's hotel, where one member denounced Patrick Kavanagh's newly published Tarry Flynn, judged obscene by the Archbishop of Dublin, as a book which would incite people to sin – " he actually said that!" She arrived home from the aspiring writers on September 5, 1946 in a black mood. "God deliver me from mediocrity!

From mediocrity in art, in vice, in virtue, in living, in dying. Why can't people do things splendidly, without thinking of impossibilities or possibilities? Why do they endure the horror of middle class existence – not life? Why do people starting off life together even set up houses on a little scale? God how I hate it."

She did well charming McManus – soon he would become features editor of Radio Eireann, commission a story for broadcast, and invite her for a studio test: decades later her voice would be familiar to millions of listeners as a regular contributor to Sunday Miscellany. By that summer of 1947 her fortunes had changed dramatically from the despair of the previous diary. The Irish Bookman printed a story and paid the glamorous sum of £3 15 shillings. Better, hugely important to her, she was proof reading the galleys of her first story accepted by the Bell, 'Girls' (reprinted with a response by Mia Gallagher in *The Writer's Torch – Reading Stories from The Bell* (2023).

She faced more civil service exams with preparatory classes at Skerry's College. "I loathe the prospect of going to Skerries and the bovine smug civil service crowd. The prospect appals me. If only I had the courage to say 'to hell with offices and becoming an established civil servant' and leave. God, if I had the courage to sink or swim by my writing."

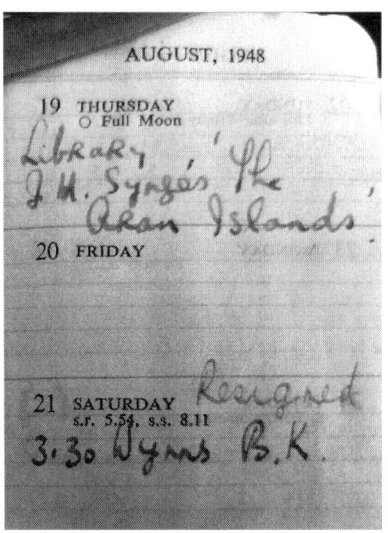

A year later, on August 21, 1948, one word in pencil in a tiny postage stamp sized diary records "resigned". On September 6 she wrote "9.30 Mail boat from Dublin". She was bound for a teaching job in Carlisle, with the half-written manuscript of *A Time Outworn* in her luggage.

She returned to Dublin in 1951, on a flood tide of mainly ecstatic reviews for *A Time Outworn*. Harper's Bazaar took an extract, commissioned a warm tribute from Frank O'Connor, accepted a short story for which they paid the staggering sum of 250 dollars, and sent one of the most famous photographers in the world, Cartier Bresson, to record the beautiful young woman in Dublin. He took her to Jammets for lunch, and embarrassed and thrilled her by sending back the wine – twice.

(O'Connor, whom she came to revere but never met, would surely have been amused to know that in December 1943 she bought two second hand copies of The Bell for six pence, and admired his article on W B Yeats, writing "making me realise that O'Connor is a much finer writer than I had realised from his stories.")

She even got the literary job, when Peadar O'Donnell looked up from his overflowing editor's desk at the Bell and said "I hear you wrote a good book". She acted as deputy editor and drama critic, with special permission to work in the afternoon and evening and stay home to write in the mornings. Unusually for those days she kept her job after her marriage to Maurice Kennedy in 1953 – the Civil Service would have booted her out. She never stopped writing and launched her memoir Friends With The Enemy in December 2017, three months before her death in March 2018, having just made her 93rd Valentine's Day.

On St Stephen's Night 1943 a poem by the 18 year old was read in a Radio Eireann broadcast she missed ("to my horror, disgust, fury and regret"). As somebody apparently commented on air that night, and as the rest of her long life proved, Val Mulkerns truly was "a remarkable girl".

Maev Kennedy
Dublin, 2024

A TIME OUTWORN

Part One

THE LAST SUMMER

Outworn heart in a time outworn
Come clear of the nets of wrong and right,
Laugh heart again in the grey twilight,
Sigh heart again in the dew of the dawn.

Your mother Éire is always young,
Dew ever shining and twilight grey,
Though hope fall from you and love decay,
Burning in fires of a slanderous tongue.

W. B. YEATS

I

Sometimes I wouldn't go home at all. I didn't that day. Even now I sometimes act on impulses like that—shying away from human contacts at the last moment. I had already failed to turn up for an appointment, and had decided to go home. But I found myself cycling out along the coast parallel with the line of dim blue mountains that hold Dublin in a loose embrace. I remember they looked vague that afternoon, muffled in grey June mist that was always on the point of lifting but never did. The sands stretched in tideless desolation for miles along to the right. I looked back, and the spires of Dublin, lifting mistily into the distance, seemed to belong to some strange city built on the edge of a desert. Mist and distance had softened away every line of familiarity. And as Dublin dimmed, Howth grew clearer, and somehow desirable.

It had been familiar to me since childhood, but it had never lost its vague lure, its atmosphere of legendary heroic dead that had once hunted boars on the hills, great tall, sandalled, laughing men with wild hair and rich Gaelic curses on their lips—Fionn and Oisín, Diarmuid and Conán and Caoilte and all the gallant band, and red star-crossed Gráinne, who had lain at last with Diarmuid there. And mingled with these in my mind were, incongruously, the lost Spanish ships that were to bring us hope, ships that sail for ever through the Irish imagination. I knew that the Western coast held more authentic, more likely memories of them, but they had been linked in my mind for longer than I could remember with the Fianna and the wild cliffs of Howth. And always as I drew nearer the little coastal town I was conscious of a quiet excitement, as if I would find at last that here was a place out of time, lightly poised between time and eternity. But the smooth wide road would lead me inevitably past the railway station, under the red smoky bridge, past the white St. Lawrence hotel, and into irrefutable reality, the strollers along the pier, the swaying fishing boats out in the bay, a woman coming out of a shop with a loaf of bread in her hand, a small boy swinging his tanned long legs up on the sea wall and paring a rod. But Howth Head, lifting above the town into the grey salty June air, with gorse lying illusively like sunlight on its slopes, still held something of the mysterious, a secret withheld from the tumbled, commonplace little town.

 I pulled up outside Geraghty's, a cheerful red homely place where they give poor teas for a reasonable price, and a great priceless sense of repose. But I was not staying for tea, and repose was not what I was seeking. I went inside to the hall and called: 'Are you there, Mrs. Geraghty?'

 'Is it Maeve Cusack that's out there? Come in, child, if it's you. And how are you? You look a bit dawny to me, but your father was only telling me the other week about the exams you were sitting, God look down on you. Sure they do have our Michael kilt too. And tell me how is your mother?'

 Mrs. Geraghty was smiling and old and spotless. She had been smiling and old and spotless when my mother was a girl, out here for tea on summer afternoons with my father. It was in the room here overlooking the bay that he had given her the engagement ring. It had cost him, he once told me, the price of a year's uneaten lunches, and she had flung it out through the open window because he had told her that too—without thinking. She had said she never wanted a ring, what was the use of it? Couldn't he have sense? And then she'd gone out to pick it up. She was tilting it to the slanting sun to see the sparkle when she came back. She was nineteen.

'She's fine, thanks, Mrs. Geraghty. Could I leave the bike here while I'm up on the Head?'

'And why wouldn't you? It'll be safe as a house there in the hall. Is it on your own you're going?'

'Yes.'

'Bedad, you're not your mother's daughter, anyway. Up the Head on your own, I ask you! That's a nice bit of white stuff in your blouse. Would that be dear now?'

'Three-and-eleven a yard,' I said. 'And thanks, Mrs. Geraghty. I don't suppose I'll be long.'

'God help you, I don't suppose you will,' said the old woman, and her dim amused eyes looked at me from under thick grey eyebrows. Long years of owning a café in Howth had made her think of life in terms of unclouded, interminable courting: couples coming down tousled and hand in hand from the heather in the cool of the evening, and sometimes untired still after the day, chancing quick tight embraces while waiting for tea to be brought in. She was proud that it was here they still came even with the new flashy cafés in town, and all her tables were for two, and in season, all had bowls of small wild roses in the centre.

I walked rather quickly past the top of the pier and struck up the steep track that went over the Head. It was a pleasant road. When you got up a bit you could see that it curved to the long shining arm of the bay, and in the mists of that afternoon the Bailey Lighthouse looked unutterably white and delicate, an ivory tower. A seagull flashed white against the grey sky above my head, and suddenly swooped so low that I could see the ugly gaping beak, shaped for the lonely cry. He cried, I fancied, into my ear and then lifted on the white wings far out on the silky misted sea. Idly I watched him glide and swoop, tilting a wing slantwise to the water, barely touching it, and then lifting again in vagrant flight, then dropping, and flashing again. It looked like some complicated dance set to a rhythm I would never know. I tired of him, and set my strong pace upward again, pulling against the hill.

Soon the little cafes with their few intimate tables for two were left behind, like gay lives I had outlived, and the little road was running wild among the heather and clumps of rock. And suddenly, as I rounded a bend, the sea coiled white and cloudy directly below, and the cliff fell steeply down to meet it, heathery, soft, dangerously inviting cliff. I had always had an inclination to sit like a child on a grassy slope, on that cliff, and slide lightly down through the heather, gathering speed until the sea seemed to rush boisterously to meet one, and then stop when the foot touched a hard barrier of rock, on the very lip of the sea.

As long as I could remember I had had that impulse, and always I stopped walking at the bend, surrendering for a few wild moments to the dream, before going on again. I stopped that day as usual, staring down along the dark purple slope that grew fainter as it neared the sea, a pale mauve glistening with mist, and suddenly merging into the cloudy white traceries of water that formed delicately around the rocks.

'If you slide down there, Maeve, you won't stop at that rock,' and like a half-awakened sleeper I glanced stupidly all around for the owner of the familiar voice. His head was jutting over the flat top of the rock above me, yellow wild hair, slightly hollowed thin cheeks with freckles, and surprisingly dark eyes. His blue summer shirt was open at the neck. There was a suggestion of strength about the throat muscles.

'Hello,' I said, without smiling. He was not smiling either, just staring with the curiously reflective dark eyes over the edge of the rock. As I stood there looking up, his eyes wandered from hair to ankle and then up again to follow my arms to the fingertips, almost like a corner-boy, except for the cool dark eyes. I scrambled up the stretch of heather to the rock and he stretched out a thin hand to pull me over the edge. I took it and stretched silently down beside him, dropping his hand once I had no further use for it. It was a soft, almost boneless hand, with narrow white fingers that curved back when the hand was outstretched, a delicate hand. We both stared hard through the thickening mist down into the sea.

'I waited for an hour outside Easons,' he said simply, at last, 'and you didn't come.' There was no question in his voice, and no accusation. He might have been beginning a story.

'No,' I said, and we were silent again. I said nothing for several minutes; then I said:

'Why did you come out here?'

'I knew you came here sometimes. When I got off the train I knew you'd come to-day. So I just came up here and waited.'

'I came because I wanted to be by myself,' I said, and the reason, given words, surprised me.

'I know,' he said, and was silent again. The only sounds were his light, untroubled breathing, and the breathing of the sea below in the mist. A seagull flashed white against the sky, perhaps the same seagull. The distant, desolate cry was the same. I thought suddenly of the days after school during the past two years when he had waited at the end of the lane for me, no matter how long I'd be. I had a vivid picture of him in his light- and dark-green school cap, sitting on his bicycle at the kerb, one dark-trousered leg on the pavement, the pile of books, which were the same as my books, strapped on the carrier of his bicycle—the Aeneid Book IV, Horace Odes II, Macbeth, and Hall and Stephens, and Tout's European History. I thought of the laughing, inquisitive remarks of the girls, charged with the curiosity of inadequate sex-knowledge. And I thought of their scattering at the end of the lane where Diarmuid Barron was waiting, and of one of them, one day, looking back and shouting:

'Diarmuid déad geal, dreach-sholuis, O'Dhuibhne,'[1] because we were doing the Fenian tales that year in school and had been told to underline that description of Diarmuid na mBan. That girl's name was Doreen Greene and already it seemed a long time ago. I shifted slightly on the hard rock, and when I looked again at my companion with head pillowed patiently on his arms, his yellow hair with the mist on it, he reminded me of that other legendary Diarmuid who had lain there too, and I had the feeling, familiar to my adolescence, of being tangled between past and present. I shook off the mood with some effort and said:

'I'm sorry, Diarmuid, but I couldn't face people, not even the family or you, so I came out here. I'm fed up. I

---

1 *Diarmuid of the bright teeth, of the sunny face, son of Dheena.*

don't know how I did in the exam, and I don't care. There isn't a chance of going on except I get a scholarship, and I know I haven't. It'll be some office job totting figures, so what's the use?'

Diarmuid gave a quick dark glance under his hair, and said nothing. His eyes were ambiguous, his hands very still on the edge of the rock.

'It's different for you,' I said, 'because your father has a shop and no children to speak of.' A laugh grew in his eyes at that, and passed slowly to his lips like the flickering light of a match. The thin mouth curved down slightly at the corners, before suddenly opening in a laugh that showed very white teeth, not quite even, that gave him a lopsided unforgettable grin. I wanted suddenly to laugh too, but his eyes never left me, and I felt compelled stubbornly to keep up the grievance that had already melted inexplicably.

'There are five of us,' I went on, ' and three still to be educated and—'

'What's a poor mother to do?' continued Diarmuid with devilment in his eyes, and a sorrowful gesture at me.

'Shut up,' I said happily, and then for no reason at all we both laughed and rolled down the rock on to the soft damp heather and lay there. It smelled good, wild and sweet and satisfying. I buried my face in it and his arm was loosely across my shoulder.

'Did you ask them if you could go to college?' I mumbled into the heather.

'Yes,' he said, tightening his arm. 'They're letting me all right, although Dad says college never sold braces or brassieres for anyone. And he's right—what's college, anyway, but an excuse for idling three or four more years?' I didn't answer, except to laugh lightly in the new-found carelessness and sit up suddenly in the heather to look at him. His yellow hair looked, like the gorse, as if sunlight were lying on it, but when I looked up through the mist I saw there was actually a rent in the woolly clouds through which slender rays of sunlight were slanting—at school the nuns used to say that these were rays of grace coming through Our Lady's fingers. I stared up at them and Diarmuid pulled heather out of my hair and said:

'If we don't get up we'll both be doubled with rheumatism before we're twenty,' and he pulled me up off the ground and I felt again the soft, slender fingers covering mine. He said:

> *Come with me under my coat*
> *And we will drink our fill*
> *Of the milk of the white goat*
> *Or wine if it be thy will.*

He always paused after the first line of that funny rapscallion poem of Stephens', and I always told him to go on. It was a ritual. After we had chorused the last line, he lifted my face with one finger and kissed me lightly on the lips. Then I kissed him and we stood still for a long time staring out to sea. The mist was lifting.

'Since there's no white goat,' Diarmuid said, 'will Mrs Geraghty's do?' and he caught my hand and we went racing down the hill through the damp heather to the little road. Mrs. Geraghty's welcome this time was quite genuine and she looked as if she were sorry for having misjudged me. After tea, we walked the nine miles back, for preference, and Diarmuid wheeled my bike with one hand.

II

It was late when I got in, perhaps half-eleven, and at first I thought everyone was in bed. Down in the warm darkness of the kitchen a tap dripped the night away—it had been dripping away the last ten years. We were always going to get a new washer, but never did. George Henderson's hat was on the hall stand and I stood for a while in the hall, the voices coming faintly through. I was half tempted to slip up to bed without going in. But that is always my first instinct when people are gathered together, and sometimes I conquer it. I slipped out of my blazer and opened the dining-room door. After the misty enchantment of Howth the room was strangely commonplace, and the domestic group was unreal—my mother under a reading-lamp, sewing the band of a tartan skirt for Bobby, my youngest sister, father with spectacles pushed up on his forehead, and leaning across from his arm-chair to George Henderson. I knew he and father were arguing; they always were. They stopped as soon as I opened the door, and I felt like a disturber of the peaceful war between them.

'Hello, everyone.'

'Hello, Maeve.'

My mother looked up from the skirt. 'Did you get your supper, Maeve? We waited till ten for you.'

'Yes,' I said defensively, because I knew she was asking where I'd been. But then I thought it would be mean to take advantage of George's being there.

'I was in Howth, and I had a meal in Geraghty's. She was asking for you. Then we walked home.'

My father and George Henderson had already taken up the fight again—I had been no serious disturbance. I dropped down on the old sofa, which sagged in the middle from years of ill-usage. But it was comfortable enough and I was tired. I was glad they didn't consider me worth bringing into the argument.

'What are they, anyway,' George Henderson was saying, 'but a bloody pack of corner-boys, the scum of Germany? Hitler was a common house painter that got an insane idea of power into his head and the idea grew like a cancer. And he poisoned everyone he met with the same idea, until there isn't a man in Germany to-day with a healthy mind, not a single man. You can't tell me anything about them.'

'I can tell you this much,' said my father, lowering his glasses and looking sternly at George through them. He has fine fierce eyes that one can never say are any particular colour, and sprouting, sandy eyebrows. 'I can tell you this much, that, sane or insane, they're giving Mr. Bloody Bull something to think about, I'm telling you they are. Bull is shaking in his shoes this minute, and near time too. Seven hundred years of oppression in this little unfortunate country and then he goes to war in defence of little Poland. We heard that one before. But Bull has something to think about now, by God he has. England is in rubble this minute. There isn't a bit of London left. Nobody except that bowsey Churchill, that was partly responsible for splitting up this country, wants the fight to go any longer. Think of Dunkirk back in '40—they ran like rabbits. Like rabbits, by God. Bull never could fight, anyway. It was Irishmen won his Empire for him, God help their sense.'

'Wait a minute now, Patsy,' George was saying ineffectually, but my father raised an overbearing hand, and his rich voice with a touch of Kerry on it, rolled out again in passionate condemnation of the Empire and the Irishmen who had won it for John Bull. From childhood I had been listening to this, until England somehow lost its identity for me as a country, and I thought of it always as a gross, treacherous, smiling man with a top hat and a prominent belly, and a whip ready to lash the Irish into subjection as soon as they lifted their heads from the ground. And similarly, I thought of Ireland symbolically, as a girl in tears by the ruins of a round tower, with a bloody slaughtered wolfhound at her feet. That was because there was such a picture, painted in vivid green and orange by my grandmother, framed and hanging on our sitting-room wall. I remember when I was very young, perhaps six, my father reading something from a thin green book that smelled sharply of mothballs, and making me repeat after him:

'But we have hidden in our hearts the flame out of the eyes of Cathleen, the Daughter of Houlihán.'

And years later, when Yeats meant more to me than he did then, I understood why my father had gone out gladly in the crazy, heroic rebellion of 1916, and why he shouted regularly at his best friend for justifying the country that had drowned our dream of a Republic in the ink of a treaty, and moreover had destroyed his own private dream of a laughing, liberated girl hunting joyously over her own hills again. But sometimes I grew tired of the eternal speech-making—I had heard it all so often before, and anyhow it was history to me, not life, as it was to him. He had seen the living passion and suffering on Pearse's face as he delivered the speech over the grave of O'Donovan Rossa. Pearse, to me, was as remotely heroic as Robert Emmet or Owen Roe. And so I was inclined to be glad when my mother glanced warningly at father and said:

'I wouldn't blame George if he never set foot in this house again.' And when I looked across at George I knew why she had spoken. His strange haggard face, so much too big for his body, was bone-white with temper, and his eyes in that setting had an unhealthy brilliance. One hand on the table was trembling. He had been partly crippled since Ypres and his heart was uncertain. I remembered suddenly all the photographs of British soldiers in his home, laughing, formal, smooth-faced young men looking at you from the piano, the mantelpiece, from every side-table. The Hendersons had fought in the British Army for generations. I was suddenly very anxious to co-operate with my mother in bringing about a truce.

'I bet you've forgotten all about the bookcase you said you'd make for my room, George,' I said, 'and the books are nearly out on the landing by now. The fuss mother makes over them you'd think they were bombs,' and I cursed the ill-chosen phrase. But George was quick to understand. He lit one of his interminable cigarettes, placed another on my father's lap, and smiled his crooked smile across at me through the smoke.

'I haven't forgotten, Maeve,' he said, 'it's nearly finished. I just want to do a bit of fretwork for the sides, that's all,' and in the storm of surprise and delight the friction was forgotten. Woodwork was one of the things that filled the crippled, tedious days for George, and he had very clever fingers. It was always for me that he made things—a dressing-table when I was twelve, because I had had to share mine with my sister Sheila; an exquisitely detailed model in bog-oak of the Custom House for my seventeenth birthday, and now a bookcase. Yet I can never remember his ever having spoken much to me—a greeting when I came in, a farewell when he was going, and an occasional casual remark when he wasn't talking to my father are all I ever remember. He seemed to have no interest in talking to anyone but my father. It wasn't long before the warrior in the corner realised what we were doing and he was wholehearted in his surrender. The fierceness died out of his eyes and they were softened in amused reminiscence under his wicked, sandy eyebrows. You could see one of the innumerable inconsequent stories taking shape in his eyes. He bent over and lit his cigarette off George's and said:

'Was I ever telling you about when I was below in Athenry forty years ago? There was an old fellow called Petey Farrell that was the richest man around—he had three of the best farms in the County Galway. But he'd frame a halfpenny rather than spend it, and he was never known to ask any man had he a mouth on him, and he was never known to drink more than a glass of plain himself. One fair day he came into Michael Dan Geraghty's pub and ordered his glass, without as much as a look at the two neighbours that were drinking at the counter. When he was finished, didn't he look up, by the way, seeing the men for the first time.

'"A fine day for the Fair, praises be to God," says he, and he on his way out.

'"It is, Petey," says one of the neighbours, "and aren't you the foolish old fellow wasting the day making more money than you haven't the heart to spend, when it's the way every third and fourth cousin of yours in the County

Galway will be lashing it around in extravagance when you'll be dead." The old man stops at the half-door and looks back over it:

'"Sure I'm willing," says he, "to let every man live according to his likes. If them that comes after me gets as much joy out of spending the money as I did out of saving it, they'll be lucky," and off he went.'

George stood up with a laugh. 'You should all have your first sleep over you by now,' he said. 'It's long after twelve.' He went out to get his hat and we all crowded into the hall to see him off. We always did that. As I watched his twisted body limping slowly down the path I had a moment's sharp pity for him. He always stayed late because for years he hadn't slept, and sometimes his eyes got tired and he couldn't read. I thought of the horror of the vacant dark hours until daylight, listening for every stir of every board in the house. Suddenly my father rushed out after him, saying he'd leave George to his own gate—that anyhow he had another thing to tell him. They went down the road together. I wondered if John Bull were getting it again. At the end of the road, across the railway bridge, a train rushed screaming by, bright carriage after bright carriage through anonymous darkness. I stood watching, idly wondering about the passing sealed lives inside.

'Are you spending the night on the doorstep, Maeve?' my mother called.

III

June was muffled in mists to the end, but in July the clouds split and shrank and floated higher in white puff balls, and for weeks our street was panelled with sun, striking yellow through the gaps between houses. The trees in the gardens—there was a surprising number of trees—dropped intricate traceries of shadow across the paths, and over in Captain Nolan's a cock shrieked all through the hot mornings a loud psalm to his virility. The Captain lived with his two brothers across the road, and was the only one around the place to keep poultry in the back garden. It was like living in the country, sometimes, to waken up in the mornings.

The Captain liked my mother—'Your mother, Maeve, is a lady, never forget that. One of the few, I regret to say, on this road '—and he let her buy as many fresh eggs as she wanted, to the intense annoyance of our neighbours. The poor man was greatly disliked, and Mrs. Greene, down the road, spent much of her time inventing libellous stories about him and his two harmless, melancholy brothers. The Captain was always complaining that no maid would stay in the house, and *she*, for one, wasn't surprised. *She* didn't have to be told the extent of the duties of any girl the Captain paid a wage to. Oh, no. He hadn't been at sea for twenty years for nothing. And the brothers were as bad. It's a wonder he didn't advertise for three maids, God help us. It would nearly be more decent.

Almost every morning Doreen, Mrs. Greene's daughter, and Nora Kiernan would call to our house, sometimes before I would be up, with bathing-suits and towels and lunch packed for a day at the sea. Nora's people had a farm in Rathfarnham, but we hardly ever went her side of the coast that summer—always to Portmarnock.

One morning when I came down to them I found Máire Lavin there too, a slight red-haired girl with innocent rounded features, and great eyes full of light. She had been at school with us too, but I think only loneliness had driven her into our company. She was simple and pious, very much out of her element in Dublin (she lived with an aunt), and I think all the fast bravado we sometimes talked shocked her. One thought of her naturally on a farm feeding calves, with a gentle Meath slope rising behind her, and morning sun on the Boyne nearby. The nostalgia you sometimes caught in her great shining eyes may have accounted for this impression. She was the sort of girl you wanted to pet like an animal, and save from any rough hands.

Portmarnock was gay and hot and vulgar—a colony of little corrugated huts strung on either side of the wide road which ran with hot, liquid tar, and beyond the last vertical hill you could see the sea, a white glittering line under the sun. Whole families evacuated out of the city to these huts in the summer, and their washing, spread on every bush, gave a touch of carnival to the place. But once you had got down on to the strand, it might have been anywhere. Sun destroys identity. This place with the stretches of sand stretched white and dazzling for miles, the indigo sea deepening at the skyline, where the heat haze pulsated, and fading into cool white waves at the edge, might just as well have been Donegal or Cannes or Brighton.

To the left Malahide Island, caught lightly in the haze, looked as enchanted as ever Mary Rose could desire. But Howth was a seal floating darkly in the sun, dreaming of mists and lost heroes. I stared across at it through eyes narrowed from the glare, as I thankfully tore off my clothes. Doreen was already in togs and she was arching her slim body backwards in what looked like a pagan act of sun worship. Her pale silky hair flowed straight from her inverted head, and her teeth showed shining for a moment. Máire Lavin was apart from us, undressing with ugly cautious movements, glancing over her shoulder and pulling the slip up another inch. It was wrong, I thought, impatiently, this graceless traditional fumbling, this terror of the human body. Nora Kiernan, who was irritated, kept making little deliberate wanton gestures, dropping a strap as if by accident and pretending not to notice. Her merry brown eyes kept winking at me, but I wasn't really amused because I pitied Máire. Suddenly I sprang across to Nora.

'If you haven't learned to do your own straps in eighteen years it's time you were shown,' and I knotted the halter neck firmly. She looked up in amazement and blinked, and I knocked her into the sand and rolled over after her. The sand was hot and soft as silk, and it moved like water to the press of our bodies. I closed my eyes in a sudden spasm of happiness—sun and sea and freedom, and the exam safely over, and life opening like a flower in my hands. Confidence welled up in me and I saw no reason in the world why I shouldn't succeed. I am always happy in the sun, and always there is that intoxicating illusion that life is in the hollow of my hand, and I am almighty.

'If we'd only a few men, now,' Doreen said, sighing. She had her idolatrous dance completed and was squatting in her white costume, with slender legs crossed like a tailor and the pale fall of hair about her face. Her skin had taken an even, honey-coloured tan, which threw up in relief the intense blueness of her eyes.

'Oh, no, it's too early,' said Nora, 'and it's too hot.'

'It's never too hot for me,' said Doreen, and her giggle pointed to the double entendre.

'You're sunk in depravity,' said Nora absently. She was taking up handfuls of sand and letting them fall glittering through her brown fingers.

'I wish I was,' said Doreen, and she rolled over on her back between Nora and me. We were all silent for several minutes. It was too hot to talk.

'Talking of men,' said Nora, as if she had introduced the subject, 'mother's giving a harvest party in September, and you're all coming. But if you want to be sure of men you'd better bring them with you, and you'd want to be very sure of them to risk one of our parties,' she added thoughtfully.

'Well, I for one am coming alone,' said Doreen, 'because I've no man to bring, and if I had six I'd still go alone, because it's more fun. What's the good of a party if you don't make contacts?'

'What's the good of a party, anyway?' said Nora. 'I hate them, but mother's crazy about them, only she'd never admit it—she keeps telling me it's for *me*. Mother's funny. You'll bring Diarmuid, won't you, Maeve?'

'No, I can't. He's on holidays in Donegal with his uncle, and he won't be back till his lectures begin in October. He's going to college,' I added redundantly.

'I expect I'll see a lot of him, so,' said Doreen.

'But he's a nice boy,' said Nora, 'so I expect you won't.'

'Your obscenity doesn't amuse me,' said Doreen. 'What's he doing, Maeve—arts?'

'Yes,' I said, and for some reason the confidence and joy drained away from me and I stared hard at Doreen for a few minutes before realising it. Then, fearful in case she'd guess what I was thinking, I said hurriedly:

'Do you like the idea of doing a degree, Doreen?' She shrugged.

'Not much—you know my capacity for application. There's only one thing I can apply myself to with any enthusiasm. It may be fun, though—they have hops and things. Did Diarmuid do the Leaving Scholarship, too, Maeve?' she added irrelevantly.

'Yes,' I said, 'but he's going, anyway.'

Doreen kicked her legs up in the air. ' What a day! ' she said. Then she sat up again. 'Did you make up your mind definitely what you're going to do, Nora?'

'No,' said Nora, 'mother did. Mother's like one of those countrywomen who get vocations for their sons, bless her. She's decided I'm going to Skerry's to do a commercial course, and when I've done it she knows a man who'll pay me money to play the typewriter for him for the rest of my natural life. I don't care—it's as good as any other job and it's better than most. He owns a sweet factory and he has pots of money and his secretary isn't satisfactory. So he's as good as promised mother the job for me. She did a line with him once when she was seventeen and he was sixteen.'

'So that's you fixed up,' said Doreen. 'What about Máire?'

We had forgotten about Máire. We were always forgetting about Máire, and I think she liked it. I remembered suddenly why I'd distracted Nora's attention. Máire was quite happily helping a small sticky child to make a sandcastle. She was turned sideways to us, and she looked well in the green wool swimsuit, with the light full on her flaming hair.

'Who, me?' she said, turning her innocent freckled face to us in the sun. 'I've got a job already. Peter's got me into the building trade, haven't you, Peter?'

Peter lifted up a scowling fat face, liberally smeared with melting chocolate. He had his wooden spade pugnaciously in his fist, like a weapon. Máire had stopped making the castle and was smiling up at him. He scowled several times from her to the neglected castle, then suddenly hit her as hard as he could across the back with his wooden spade and raced away over the sand. But he tripped on something and fell sprawling on his face, and anyone with reasonably good ears could have heard his screeches a mile away. We were delighted. But Máire sprang to the rescue and arrived just after the horrible child's mother, who carried him off howling. Máire came back to us laughing across the sands.

'He was sweet,' she said, dropping down beside us, and we were convulsed with laughter.

'What a woman!' said Nora in despair.

'What a kid!' said Doreen.' What an abominable, unclean little monster! I know what you're going in for, anyway—dry nursing.'

'Dry nursing?' Máire's smile was wide, charming, immutably innocent. 'Do you know what, I was just thinking, and you all talking, how queer it is for us all to be left school? Isn't it queer, though?'

'Queer? We're all eighteen—how much longer do you want us to stay?' Doreen jumped up and made several attempts to stand on her hands, all of them unsuccessful.

Looking down into Máire's great cloistral, luminous eyes, I suddenly saw what she meant, and it seemed strange to me too. A whole world had passed away, a safe world of order, and the smell of fresh linen, and incense, and books, and freshly pared pencils, a world of cool, high corridors, and bells, and the rustle of rosaries, a world we had known since childhood. We had always struggled against its restrictions, and thought we hated them, but now I suddenly felt as if a foothold I'd thought was there had been removed.

'I'm going for a swim,' I said, jumping up. 'Race you all there!' Doreen easily won and I was behind her. As soon as I had plunged I felt the old, sensual delight of a half-naked body giving itself to the sea, and the vague nostalgia for lost things dissolved with the first few strokes. Life was good, and the sun was shining, and we were young. I suddenly remembered one day during the previous summer when we were out cycling in Kildare. We had stopped at a grassy bank where two old men were resting, pulling at their pipes in the sun. 'Is this the way to Oughterard, please?'

''Tis so,' said one of them, 'but 'tis a bad divil of a rocky road,' and we said thanks, and were starting off again when he turned to the other old man and said:

'But sure what does the likes of them care no more than young lepping goats?' It was true, I thought, turning over on my back and lying on the smooth swell of water. What did we care?

IV

Diarmuid wrote from Donegal: 'I see from the papers that some new company is doing Yeats's *The Countess Cathleen* at the Abbey—we were neither born nor thought of the last time that was done. I wish to God I could get down for it, but the fare down and back (mother insists on my staying here till October) is about double what I have at the moment, and there isn't anyone I can ask. Do you remember last year when we read it together on a succession of rainy afternoons in Toni's? Remember the hiss of the ice-cream soda which called forth my unpardonably Rabelaisian remark? But you could buy fourpenny fruit drinks and stay there the whole afternoon, and wasn't that all we cared about? (I have the doubtful consolation that you'll never marry me for my money, Maeve.) For God's sake don't miss it—even if you have to vamp somebody to take you—and write to me that night when you get home and tell me about it. Do you still love Aleel's lines that you used to make me say over and over again, in the hiss of the ice-cream soda?

> *Old woman, old woman,*
> *You robbed her of three minutes' peace of mind,*
> *And though you live unto a hundred years,*
> *And wash the feet of beggars and give alms,*
> *And climb Croagh Patrick, you shall not be pardoned.'*

I did still love them, and I wouldn't have missed the play for a good deal. I remember the air of excitement in the small green foyer—excitement perhaps nearly as great as on the very first night, in the Ancient Concert Rooms in 1899. Only the play was late news then, the subject of a furious controversy between clergy and artist, whereas now it was legend, aureoled with the vague romance and nostalgia common to all legends. Then, too, the poet Yeats was the excited producer of the play, with already great dreams of a National Theatre maturing in his head, whereas now in the foyer of that theatre he was only a memory and a portrait hung high in the entrance, with the summer light falling mellow on the noble, dreaming face, the lips smiling with the merest twist of irony. And there, I thought, was the link between the two performances, as I watched an old woman being helped into the theatre. She was 'Madame,' for whom the play had been written, for whom a thousand enduring images had been created. It was hard to think of her now as the beautiful girl who had played like a flame through all the early poetry, who had carried the wild summer in her gaze. But it was easy to think of her as the symbol of a nation's resurrection, the Old Woman in Cathleen Ní Houlihán who, with a turn of her head and a falling back of the shawl, could be a young girl with the walk of a queen.

All this passing through my mind, I stood with my brother and sister waiting for the gong. Brendan had wanted to see the play, and Sheila had been sent along by my mother in the hope that it would 'civilise her a bit.' Sheila had set out to be bored with an air of generous resignation—she was a healthy, dark, heedless girl of sixteen, with large laughing eyes, and she never looked dressed without a camogie stick in her hand. She was murderous on the field.

'Who's that old one?' she asked, in her loud, cheerful voice.

'Shut up, Sheila,' I said disagreeably. Brendan looked carefully around to see if she'd heard.

'That's Maud Gonne,' he said.

'Oh!' said Sheila. The name meant nothing to her and she had not the slightest desire that it should ever mean more. She let her eyes play vacantly over the audience and made a restless, bored, clicking sound with her tongue against the roof of her mouth. Brendan looked up at me and grinned. He had a pleasant grin which transformed the dark, worried, clerk's face. And then the first gong sounded and we went in.

For me the excitement of that night was something new and exotic. I had always thought of poetry as a private thing, or at the most, something to be enjoyed with one other person, and a particular person at that. But these actors had caught the exalted lyrical mood of the play so that it was overflowing on to a whole audience, and Yeats's characters were coming gradually and beautifully to life, taking us away from the twentieth century into the shadowed world of medieval Ireland in a time of famine. The starving peasants are selling their souls for gold to two wandering devil-merchants, and the young Kathleen, their ruler, strikes a bargain and sells her soul so that her people may be saved, and in that direct dramatic situation Yeats throws all the shining forces of heaven against the powers of hell. And the complicated, delicate verse-rhythms build up the mood to an almost unbearably exciting climax, the curtain-lines of the third act, when Cathleen, having made her heroic resolution, is standing poised, as she believes, on the brink of hell:

> *Mary, Queen of Angels,*
> *And all you clouds on clouds of saints, farewell!*

And the curtain falls on her despair, the hushed voice, the taut body, the wide eyes 'more beautiful than the pale stars.' The young actress was astonishingly good, bringing to the part a delicate, flame-like intensity that kept the play all the time on Yeats's high poetic level.

But somehow, leaving the theatre, individual performances faded and it was the poet's world of enchanted, imperishable beauty that clung. It was the fantastically lovely word-music that was still ringing in my ears.

> *He bids me go*
> *Where none of mortal creatures but the swan*
> *Dabbles, and there you would pluck the harp, when the trees*
> *Had a heavy shadow about our door,*
> *And talk among the rustling of the reeds,*
> *When night hunted the foolish sun away*
> *With stillness and pale tapers.*

We came out of the theatre into reality and the streetlamps of Abbey Street struggling palely with the summer twilight. Brendan was quiet and I was mentally composing the letter to Donegal. Both of us had forgotten Sheila, almost.

'What do you think of it, Sheila?' I said at last.

'If you want to know, I think it's all lies,' said Sheila.

V

I was almost asleep that night, the letter safely written, when Brendan opened the door softly and put his head in. I could see him in the triangle of light from the landing, the monkish pale face, the dark-rimmed spectacles, the untidy fall of black hair.

'Are you asleep, Maeve?'

'No. I mean nearly. You can come in.' I clicked on the light behind me and he came across and sat on the end of the bed. Nocturnal visits like this were not unusual. Sometimes he only came in to tell me incredibly poor jokes, when he wasn't feeling like sleep. He indicated Sheila lying curled in bed beside me, her hair plaited, her face mysterious in sleep.

'Is she asleep?'

'Yes. She's been asleep for ages.'

'She was probably asleep in the theatre.'

'Probably.' I wished he'd go. I had been concentrating on something I hoped I'd dream. But Brendan just sat there, thin, restless, polishing his spectacles needlessly in the corner of the sheet. I looked at his reflection in the mirror opposite—from that angle he looked rather like an overworked clerical student, stooped in the dark clothes, the pale face haggard.

'Did I ever tell you the one about the drunk in the DTs?' He put on the spectacles.

'No.' He had.

'Well, this fellow came into a pub one day, and a

pink elephant came in too and sat on the stool next him. The man ordered a whisky, and the pink elephant tapped him meaningly on the shoulder. "Here," said the man, "I don't mind your following me around wherever I go, but I draw the line at buying you whiskies." Go on, laugh. Very hot.'

I laughed at the look on Brendan's face. The funny thing is that he always sees how bad the jokes are. He took off the spectacles again.

'Did you waken me up to tell me that?'

'You weren't asleep.'

'I nearly was. Well, did you?'

'No.'

'All right. I'm listening.'

'Stop staring at me like that, woman. You'd think I never came in before. You're making me nervous.'

'I'm not *making* you.'

'You are.'

'Who says? Ah, hell, good night.'

'Good night.'

He went as far as the door and came back. 'You know that friend of yours. The one with red hair.'

'Máire Lavin?'

'Yes, her. Is she doing a line with anybody?'

'No. Good Lord, no.'

'Why not? Why shouldn't she? She's better looking than you are.' His eyes were annoyed and bright behind the spectacles—my father's eyes.

'I know, but—well, you don't know her, that's all.'

'I know I don't, but that isn't my fault. I'd like to know her. In fact, I want to know her.'

'But you don't like girls—you always said you didn't.'

'I always said I didn't like Doreen and most of your

friends, and I always said I hated the girls in the office. Who wouldn't? Hags. But I'm not so dumb as not to see the difference in Máire.'

'What brought her into your head to-night, though? You haven't seen her for a week.'

'I dunno. The play, maybe. Countess Cathleen reminded me of her—a kind of innocence, or something.'

'I see. What do you want me to do? Lock you into the drawing-room with her some night?'

'Shut up. It's not funny. Can you not think of anything?' I laughed at him over the top of the sheet, but I was only rousing him. The thing seemed to me perfect.

'I know. Nora's people are giving a party in September—the first Sunday—and Máire will be there. Would you come?'

'Just try me,' he said. He hated parties.

'All right,' I said. 'I'll fix it.'

'You're a decent kid. Good night.'

'Good night.'

He went over to the door again and came back.

'Are you sure you can fix it without saying anything, Maeve?'

'No. How could anyone fix anything without saying something?'

'You're a bloody awful woman sometimes.'

I laughed at him again, the worried scholar's face, the helplessness of him.

'You won't say anything, though, Maeve. Sure you won't?'

'No. I won't say anything.'

'And you'll fix it so I'll be asked?'

'Yes.'

'Okay. Good night.'

'Good night.'

He went to the door again and I half expected a third return. But he went out and closed the door very softly. Then I heard the door of his own room closing softly too, and in the stillness I heard faintly the dripping tap down in the kitchen. Long years of it had softened away all irritation, and the sound was as soothing as a little stream running over pebbles through the night. I turned out the light, and lay there happily in the darkness, smiling at the complicated delicacy of human relationships. But gradually a human face pushed away every other thought and floated dreamily beside mine on the borders of sleeping and waking. And Sheila, warm and curled and dreaming beside me, turned over and said in her sleep: ' Run, you fool, run! Oh run!'

VI

I was walking down O'Connell Street one day in the rain when I met Maureen O'Grady, fuzzy, excited, and lisping, in a blue raincoat.

'They're out, Maeve, did you know? My brother heard they were and he rang up, and they said they'd been sent to the school, and I went up to school this morning, and I got it, honestly, *would* you believe it, Maeve?' I wouldn't have believed it—woolly-headed, gossipy Maureen, who had spent the whole of her schooldays eating apples and copying other people's exercises. But I was glad.

'That's marvellous, Maureen, congrats. You didn't hear about anyone else, did you?'

'Yes. I think Nora, and Vera—no, I don't think they did. I forget. But imagine *me*, Maeve! I was to meet my sister at a quarter-past to tell her, and it's half-past now. 'Bye, Maeve. Sure, don't you know you've got it?' I knew nothing of the kind, but she was gone.

Twenty minutes later I was in one of the parlours in the convent, sitting in my damp, grubby raincoat, waiting for the Mistress of Studies to arrive. The rain had stopped, and long fingers of watery cowslip sunshine were coming in from the Georgian street and resting still and bright on the mahogany table. That table had supported generations of refractory schoolgirl elbows—it had often supported mine. One was sent here for any offence committed in the classroom. It was a room alive with memories for me, amusing frozen memories of my early teens. An old wise nun with brilliant blind eyes feeling my face and saying: ' What's bred in the bone, Maeve. Tell your mother I said that, won't you, Maeve. She'll know well what I mean. She was often here herself. One day she was here for hitting Mother Prioress in the face with ink-pellets shot from a ruler. What's bred in the bone, Maeve. What did they send you here to-day for, child?'

'For taking off my stockings in class, sister.'
'And what did you do that for, Maeve?'
'For a dare, sister. And it was too hot, sister.'
'So you didn't much mind taking the dare, Maeve?'
'No, sister. But I always take dares, sister.'

And when Mother Prioress had come in afterwards to deliver the long lecture on modesty I had let my eyes stray around the room in agonised boredom—the lovely repose of Raphael's heavily framed Madonna of the Chair, the sun slicing through the Venetian blinds and flowing along the dark, rich table, the shadowed twisted figure of the crucified Christ above the mantelpiece, the huddled books in the corner case near the door, and all the time my own voice saying 'Yes, mother,' and 'No, mother,' without having the least idea what it was admitting, what denying. How many years ago was all that—five, six? The smell of this parlour was the same, the smell of all convents—fresh linen, and candles, and waxed floors and old wood.

And then the Mistress of Studies was in the room, diminutive, smiling, with tiny new dentures from a face pale as a candle. The results sheet was in her hands—small, dry, rather beautiful hands—and the dull large eyes were fixed on my face. She shook hands, almost as if I were a distinguished visitor, and said in the small ticking voice:

'Congratulations, Maeve. You are welcome. Nothing to be ashamed of here.'

'Thank you, Mother.'

I glanced across the sheet as she held it, and suddenly, as if someone had shouted it, I knew it was no good. The marks were good, but they were not good enough. I did not look up.

'Your History is excellent, Maeve—your marks were the highest in the school, and your English and Latin and Irish—'

But I wasn't listening. What did I care about my History or Latin or anything else? As far as I was concerned I had failed in what I'd set out to do. The small, unreal voice ticked on, and I lifted my eyes from the sheet to the frail, dry hands that for forty years had touched only rosaries and fresh linen and children's copy books—passionless hands. I can't remember if I found anything to say to her, or if I even said good-bye, but I remember the handsome black cat that looked at me outside in the street, the waxed, glistening whiskers, the immortal mockery in his steady, green eyes.

A week later there was a letter from Diarmuid saying he had got the scholarship.

VII

After a great deal of consideration Mrs. Kiernan had decided to make the party a dress affair. Evening-dress parties were rather unusual in Dublin, so perhaps that was why. She was a magnificent, tall, expansive woman, with a bosom unsteady as an overblown tea-rose, and misleadingly intelligent dark eyes, only a little less bright than her jewellery. She had a loud, bawdy laugh, and a mouth that was good-natured and naively sensual. Her generosity was incalculable. It was dangerous to admire anything in the house because she would think nothing of giving one a valuable ornament, or a cushion, or a pretty side-table, or anything one might admire from her overflowing jewel-box. She got violent and unmanageable if one refused. She demanded in return only complete submission, even from friends of her daughter, or casual acquaintances. Her family—Nora and Mr. Kiernan—had long ago, I believed, surrendered their independence because their energy was less boundless than hers, and they would get tired of resisting long before she would tire of forcing. And so Nora was an earlier, prettier, more intelligent and less strong-willed edition of her mother, and Mr. Kiernan was an obediently cheerful little man of sixty, with anxious eyes and a great willingness to be of service to his wife, daughter, their friends, or any of the three farmhands. His wife chose his clothes, as she chose Nora's, and the clothes of anyone else who would let her. On several occasions she told Doreen and me that the next frock we'd get should be red or yellow, and that young girls like us should go in more for tight bodices—we wouldn't always be young and worth looking at, look at *her*. Doreen was considerably impressed, and always wore tight jumpers visiting the Kiernans. Cussedness made me wear my floppiest blouses, and I think she considered me a fool. Whenever Máire Lavin came in for any of this advice, her lovely, innocent face was something of a distraction to Mrs. Kiernan. Máire would keep the great eyes wonderingly on her all the time, like a child seeing its first giraffe at the zoo.

The house, 'Springfield,' was big and old and very ugly from the outside, like most houses in County Dublin. It had white steps up to the door and was long and rather narrow, with a square porch and the tall heads of poplars showing behind the house. The outhouses and stables were all to the right, from the road, which gave a slightly lopsided effect. But the long tree-lined drive up to the house was beautiful, and the little sham Gothic lodge was delightfully incongruous and gave a faintly exotic air to the place. Mountains rose up on all sides in the foreground and background, the low, wooded Dublin Hills very close, the blue-shadowed Wicklow Mountains lifting behind them

The house had been built in the second half of the last century, when neither building-material nor space was of any consequence. Mr. Kiernan's father, even with his fourteen children and four servants, could never have found use for all the rooms, but he had furnished all of them, and most of the furniture was still there, covered by dust sheets in big, unused rooms. There was an amusing story of Lucy, the first girl of that family who had wished to break away for the purpose of matrimony.

After several years' persuasion, old Kiernan had agreed to the marriage, but immediately after the ceremony he had informed the bridegroom that the house in Baggot Street did not meet with his approval, and that he would give the young man a year in which to fit it suitably. During that year Lucy would remain in Springfield with her people. Furthermore, it would be unsuitable for a child to be born among so many younger and innocent girls, and therefore to provide against such a possibility, the marriage could not be consummated until the end of the year. There were tears and storms, but old Kiernan was invincible and Lucy's young man was apparently open to persuasion, and certainly not over-passionate. The outcome was that Lucy returned to Springfield and her husband to the unsuitable house in Baggot Street. They were to see each other at lunch in Springfield every Sunday. I've often wondered about those Sundays. There was a photograph of Lucy down in the enormous, flagged kitchen. She was a small girl, with pale hair knotted high on her head, wide timid bright eyes, and the most indomitable mouth I've ever seen. I fancy she did not waste a great many Sundays in futile tortures of desire, even if her husband was spineless. That wonderful mouth in the photograph suggested numerous illicit journeys to the orchard or up among the unused bedrooms. At least, I hoped so.

    Mrs. Kiernan had decided that Doreen, Máire, and I would go out to the house in the early afternoon to help with the party preparations, and the prospect of bringing out our things and dressing together in Nora's big bedroom appealed to all of us. And we gathered that there would not be a great deal of work to be done, even with only one maid. In this we were wrong.

The three of us arrived together to find Mrs. Kiernan enthusiastically directing operations, dressed apparently for the party, except for her short dress. Her jewellery was profuse and recklessly chosen, her hair freshly dyed and gathered into a riot of curls on top of her head. She was happy. Her eyes were brilliant with excitement as she rushed around from Nora to the maid, Maisie, and from Maisie to Mr. Kiernan. Each of these people was trying patiently to carry out the violently contradictory orders.

'Now, Maisie, the hall's to be polished first. You stick to cutting bread, Nora—and *thinly*, Nora—for the sandwiches, and John, you might see about getting in some lettuce. Nora, go out with your father and see he only takes the heads with good white hearts, and Maisie, you could wash your hands and slice tomatoes and see about breadcrumbs for the ham—maybe Mr. Kiernan would help you to grate them, or Nora.'

As soon as we appeared—through the kitchen door around the back—she rushed to welcome us and kissed us all tirelessly.

'You're lovely—you all look gorgeous, and it's nothing to what you'll look to-night. I'll have to see your dresses first—don't forget the lettuce, John, and run down to Mrs. Keogh and ask her to send the young one up to help—come up and show us them in my room. Come on up.'

And she marched us up the stairs and across the wide first landing to her room, a place made hideous by the conflict of unfriendly perfumes. She hustled the dresses out of our cases and held up the folds of them to the light, and when she'd finished looking at one she'd let it drop to the ground and rush at the next. We picked our dresses patiently off the floor and listened to her.

'It's gorgeous, Maeve darling, gorgeous. Did your mother make it?'

'No,' I said, nettled. 'It was bought. It's an advance birthday present.'

'Lovely, lovely. And yours, Doreen, is a real little peach. A few splashes of perfume now where the neck ends'—Doreen's neckline was one after Mrs. Kiernan's own heart—'and you'll be all right for the night. It's the sly little splash of perfume that does it—look, you can have some of mine, I've pints to spare. Take this now, Doreen darling, in case you forget. I don't mind a bit—didn't I tell you I'd pints, more than I'll ever use?' (Mrs. Kiernan did herself an injustice.) 'And yours, Máire, is lovely too—like a First Communion dress, isn't it? It's lovely. She might do better in it than either of you,' she ended, turning to Doreen and me with her guttural, ambiguous laugh.

Another girl might have been annoyed—although there was no malice in Mrs. Kiernan—but Máire laughed good-humouredly and said it would be a change, because she never 'did well' at parties, although she always enjoyed them. And I suddenly remembered that I'd said nothing to her about Brendan, although I had got him invited all right.

'It's about time we were getting down to give a hand,' I said, and Mrs. Kiernan jumped as if she'd been stung.

'Sure, I was nearly forgetting all about them downstairs, and declare to God they're like babies when I'm not there to tell them what to do—if I don't remember everything, it's God help us,' and she was off again, across the landing and down the stairs, like a falling trunk. We followed more leisurely, and coming down the stairs I took Máire's arm.

'Brendan's coming to the party to-night, Máire, and I want you to be nice to him.'

'Me?' said Máire. 'I'm sure he wouldn't be bothered with me, when Doreen, and Nora, and all the others are here.'

'But he would, Máire. I know he would, and don't freeze him, will you?'

Her large innocent eyes caught all the light from a long window we were passing, and the reflected glow on her clear, ivory skin (common to people of her colouring) somehow gave the same effect as sunlight on the stone angel-faces in our church.

'But I never freeze people, Maeve,' she said, slightly worried. 'Why should I? And Brendan's a very nice boy. Of course I'll be nice to him, if I get the chance, but he'll be much too busy to notice me,' and she smiled her beautiful untroubled smile, that brought the stone angels into my mind again.

'You wait and see,' I said, and my amused tone brought back the perplexed expression to her face, and her eyes were unhappy. I pulled her red, long hair. 'Never mind me,' I said. 'Let's go and get orders, though it might be better if we gave them. Isn't she a terror?'

'I know,' said Máire, 'but she's the most generous woman I ever met, and she doesn't mean half what she says.'

If it had been anyone else I would have replied immediately: 'You mean she doesn't say half what she means,' but as it was I agreed, and we went down into the cool long kitchen where Lucy's grave eyes watched the preparations from the wall.

Somehow, despite Mrs. Kiernan and because of the lodge-keeper's wonderful daughter aged twelve, the preparations went on well, and by six o'clock everything was ready, and there were bowls of late roses everywhere, and in a large alcove in the hall (it used to be a fireplace) there was an oval vase of flame-tipped, yellow chrysanthemums.

And then Mrs. Kiernan delighted us all by producing her last-minute surprise, a collection of lovely Chinese lanterns which she sent one of the men to hang from trees near the house, and we suspended several in the hall porch, one at each corner. It looked like the setting for a harlequinade, and we wondered what the place would look like at dusk, when the lanterns would be lighted. There would be scores of them indoors too, because electricity had never been installed in Springfield. Mrs. Kiernan said it was vulgar. The light would be provided by candles, a few oil-lamps, and the lanterns. It was all highly dangerous, of course, but nobody thought of that, and I'd always loved the effect of the unfamiliar Springfield lighting. It seemed natural for an old house so near Sarah Curran's ruined home.

At about eight o'clock (the guests were to arrive at nine) the four of us went up to dress. It was not really dark, there was just a thickening of the autumn air; and down in the city, a few lights shone and disappeared— people looking for things in dusky rooms, perhaps. But the light was too vague for the important business of dressing, and Nora struck a match and lit the branching candelabrum in the middle of her dressing-table. The three flames were pale as flowers in their conflict with daylight, but they threw a clear pool of light on the centre mirror, and slightly lit the two swinging side mirrors. The dresses had all been carefully laid on the bed, after Mrs. Kiernan's excited ill-treatment of them, and I stood vaguely looking at them as they lay fresh and anonymous on the quilt. Parties, with their sense of unnaturally heightened life, usually depress me.

'You'd better start kicking off your things soon, Maeve, or you'll be last ready, and that's unlucky,' Doreen said.

She was laughing under the edge of her evening dress; it was just being slipped over her head. It was silver and had a slit from knee to hem, through which you saw the movement of a rounded, silky leg. The bodice was slit too, almost to the waist, and a diamond clasp held the edges together at the throat. It made her pale hair look almost silver, and smooth as water, and her eyes too were water, blue in sunlight. She glittered, and turned in front of the glass, smiling at her reflection in the candlelight.

'Is it lucky to be first, Doreen?' I said.

'I don't know. Anyhow, I don't need luck,' she said. It was things like this that made some people dislike her. 'And anyhow, I'm not first. Look at Nora.'

Nora already had on her flame-coloured dress and was struggling to fasten the last button down the back.

'I'll do that for you, Nora,' said Máire from the corner. As she ran across the carpet in her bare feet she looked, as Mrs. Kiernan had hinted, very like a First Communicant in her guileless white dress, with the red hair falling about her shoulders. When she turned to the candles to say something to Doreen, each eye held a flame.

There was some competition for the mirrors when it came to doing our hair, but finally we agreed that Nora should have the centre one (the room being hers) and Doreen and I should have a side mirror each. Máire said that the wardrobe mirror would do for all she was going to do with her hair. We worked silently for a few moments as the early dusk thickened outside. Nobody had thought of drawing the curtains. Suddenly Doreen swung around from the mirror and said:

'I've never been so excited in my *life* about any party. It's the evening dresses or something. I don't know what. But I feel—' and she dropped her comb and swung her arms above her head, and didn't say what she felt.

But we knew. The shining dress and hair and eyes had infected us too with her strange excitement, and it was as if flames had suddenly been fanned within us. Nora spun on her heel and sent the scarlet wide skirt coiling in an arc, dangerously near the candles. Máire came over and caught her around the waist until she stopped, and dropped laughing on the bed. She pulled Máire with her.

'Know what,' said Doreen, glittering beside the mirror. 'I've a marvellous idea. Let's make a pact that we'll *all* get men to make love to us to-night. That's the way I'm feeling, and if you'd all only admit it—'

'I never denied it,' said Nora from the bed.

'Nor I,' I said.

'Well,' said Doreen, 'that's settled. Anyone who doesn't get a man'll have to treat the rest of us to a show. Is that fixed, Máire?'

'Yes,' said Máire unhappily, looking at her silver shoes. But I knew it wouldn't be she who would have to treat us.

'It won't be me, anyhow,' said Doreen. 'I could handle St. Thomas this minute.' The story had often been told us at school: St. Thomas Aquinas seizing a burning torch and chasing the naked sorceress out of his cell, and cutting the sign of the cross in flames on the closed door.

'Even the certainty of scorching wouldn't put me off,' she added. 'Who's coming anyway, Nora?'

'Oh, everyone. The Moore boys and Maeve's brother and the Cronins and Garret Hurley—you probably don't remember him—he's been away in the war for ages. His people live around here. And then there's the crowd we knew in school. I asked all of them, only Diarmuid's away, of course. Is that enough to be going on with?'

'Oh yes,' Doreen said carelessly, 'that will do. You know, Maeve, I like Brendan. He has a nice studious face and he tells you very funny stories all the time—so unexpected. I think *him*,' she added thoughtfully, swinging one leg through the slit in her dress.

Máire looked up at me with quick amusement in her eyes, and I winked back.

'You can try,' I said, 'but you never know with Brendan. He has peculiar taste,' and when Doreen looked happily into the mirror I smiled across at Máire again. She smiled vaguely back, a rather clouded smile.

'Never mind,' said Doreen, shining at us, 'when I *want* something—and in this dress too. I mean I don't see how he can, do you, Nora?'

'No,' said Nora, 'I don't. Do you want a rose, Maeve? Mother left some over there for us.'

'I'd love one,' I said. 'A red one, I think.'

She chose a fresh opening bud from the bowl and threw it across the room. Máire caught it neatly as it went over her head and came over to pin it in for me. She had neat, willing fingers. I looked up at her hair, glorious behind the candles. Doreen was looking out through the window.

'A car,' she said. 'I can see the lights—do you think it's Brendan, Maeve?'

'If it was a bus, it might be Brendan,' I said. 'Do you think he'd bother coming in a taxi when he's alone?'

'Well, anyhow, I'm going down,' said Doreen. 'The time to get intimate with people is in the *beginning* of a party. Anybody coming?' She looked lovingly at herself for the last time and ran a satisfied hand from throat to thigh.

'Are we all ready?' said Nora, her face, in excitement, very like her mother's. We all were, but we lingered, like children who look at sweets a long time in their hands before biting them, reluctant to bring the last bite nearer. Nora lifted her hand like a blessing: 'Good luck, ladies,' she said, and she pushed us all out of the room and followed us downstairs. The hired band (saxophone, piano, and violin) was tentatively trying the first dance tune of the night, and it rose to a crescendo of vulgar grief as we reached the hall.

The hall door was open, and out in the porch the Chinese lanterns swung dreamily, and threw a coloured twilight. It was almost dark. Somewhere, someone banged the door of a car, and we stood huddled at the coiled foot of the staircase, waiting for the first face at the door. Máire unaccountably slipped her hand through mine. And then, like an exploded firework, Mrs. Kiernan burst out of one of the far rooms, and the vague uncertainty we had all been feeling was dissolved.

'You're pictures, the whole lot of you, I declare to God. Pictures. Come out, John, till you see them, and leave that whisky alone—it's not an execution you're going to—will you look who's here! How are you, Paddy and Sean and Oliver? You're welcome,' and she was off in a bounce to the door, an impressive vast figure in tight black satin, which foiled the massed jewellery.

The three boys came in, smiling and rather shy—the

Moore boys. And then several girls with dresses caught up, ran up the steps, and we took charge of them, taking them to the large room full of mirrors which had been set aside as a dressing-room. Mr. Kiernan, smiling and anxious, his fingers still tingling for the whisky bottle, came out and took the boys away to remove their coats. From that on there were people arriving all the time, the large family of Cronins with their parents (the Cronin girls all giggled and all had prominent front teeth and the Cronin boys were mostly handsome), Garret Hurley and his sister, and several bald, joking men who had been youthful friends of Mrs. Kiernan, and at last I saw Brendan coming rather dazedly from under the Chinese lanterns, as if he had lost his way to the cloister. He looked well in evening dress, which showed up to advantage his rather startling black-and-white colouring. He had spent hours brushing his hair, I guessed, and it shone like coal. Mrs. Kiernan received him rapturously, shaking his hands and whispering impressively into his ear. As soon as she released him I rushed over.

'Hello, Bren. Look, if you wait one minute I'll get Máire and ask her to show you where to leave your things. And it's up to you to hold on to her. I take no responsibility after this.'

'Who asked you to?' he grinned. 'Thanks, Maeve. Oh God, Maeve, look at Doreen's dress!'

I found Máire in the cloakroom among the girls, helping people to fix their hooks, and comb their hair, and arranging flowers for them.

'I want you in the hall, Máire,' I said, taking her hand and detaching her from one of the Cronin girls, whose suspender she was adjusting. She came with me reluctantly, and I told her Brendan wanted to be shown around.

'Oh Maeve! ' she said unhappily, turning the great eyes imploringly on me. 'You know how stupid I am with boys—I won't know what to say,' and she looked wildly around for escape. But I kept her hand firmly in mine, and we found Brendan where I had left him, blinking a little behind the dark-rimmed spectacles.

'Here she is, Brendan,' I said. 'She'll show you—I'm too busy.' And suddenly Brendan's glance was steady and shining and humble, and he said:

'You don't mind, Máire? If I may say so, you look very sweet in white'—and I thought: Oh, the fool! the fool!

But Máire, amazingly, didn't seem to mind, and she smiled at him and innocently took his arm, steering him through the crowd and up the wide staircase to the first landing. They stood out among all the coloured crowd, he in black-and-white, she in white, like a bride and groom, I thought, as I watched them moving up the stairs. They came under a swinging lantern for a moment, and her hair blazed red-gold against the white dress. She was laughing, in profile, and so was Brendan.

Gradually everyone drifted into an enormous high room full of golden light from the chandeliers, and full of sad music from the band. The three musicians were in a curtained alcove at the top of the room (it, too, had once been a wide fireplace—there had been three fireplaces in the room), but their music was everywhere, (the weeping music to which we dance. But nobody was dancing yet. The room was full of chatting groups, smoking and drinking a little, and laughing a great deal—party laughter. Trays of drinks were going around. There was champagne. Girls in gay, mildly inviting dresses looked over the rims of their glasses, and joyously weighed their prospects for the night. The young Moores were losing their shyness, and each had already acquired a girl—the youngest of them was sitting on a pouffe at Doreen's feet, gazing ardently up along the length of silver at her face, and Doreen was looking anxiously over his head to where Brendan sat with Máire, telling her jokes probably, because they were both laughing. And through all the groups, like a summer thunderstorm in black satin, rolled Mrs. Kiernan, laughing, encouraging, fixing partnerships for the night, and drinking a glass with everybody. Suddenly she moved over to Mr. and Mrs. Cronin, flung her bare arms around both of them, and said something. Mrs. Cronin shook her tightly-waved head and backed away to the wall, and the next thing was Mrs. Kiernan and Mr. Cronin arranged themselves for the dance, and lumbered heavily across the floor in an attempted foxtrot. They were encouraged by a patter of handclapping and a loud lonely blast from the saxophone. Mr. Cronin blinked uncertainly, but manfully, in the glare of the jewellery, and danced at a discreet distance from the sprawling, unsteady bosom.

And then things began to happen. More and more couples took courage, and some—including Doreen and her young Moore—were graceful dancers, within the range of the foxtrot. Boys, shy until now, walked across the floor in their formal suits and took up the owners of eyes which had invited over the rims of wine-glasses. Nora's scarlet dress was whirling around the legs of a shapely young Cronin—Harry Cronin, and Brendan and Máire were dancing with grave concentration, Máire's chin resting quietly on his shoulder as if it had never known any other support. I was dancing soberly with one of the bald former boyfriends of Mrs. Kiernan—he kept begging me to call him Teddy, and reeked of brandy. Was it unlucky to have been the last dressed? At the end of the dance I took Teddy across firmly and introduced him to Mrs. Cronin, and left them talking about their appendices. They danced the next slow waltz, carefully and with restraint, as befitted people who had two internal organs missing. I slipped out into the cool hall, and played vaguely with the chrysanthemum petals. Somebody touched my arm.

'Hello. I couldn't get to you before grandfather for that dance. Do you remember me, Maeve?' I did—Garret Hurley. He was a tall boy of twenty-two, with a cultured bored voice, and curiously sated eyes. The satiety was now mingled with a vast indifference, as of someone who has looked unblinking over the rim of hell, and can never again be scared by anything. But his smile had not changed, weak and eagerly confiding like a child's.

'Of course,' I said. 'It's nice seeing you again. Are you home on leave?'

'Sick leave.'

'You don't look sick.'

'No,' he said, bored with the subject. 'Do you remember the last time I saw you, Maeve, at another party here? You were fourteen and I was eighteen. You drank orange squash all night and sang "Let Erin Remember."'

'And you drank port all night and wouldn't sing anything. And you were sick on the carpet.'

'Yes,' he said. 'It's a long time ago.'

'Four years.'

'It's a long time ago,' he repeated, smiling with his lips only. 'Shall we dance?'

'Yes. I'd love to.'

He danced well, with smooth, controlled movements;

the sort of dancer who steers a smooth course through the most crowded ballroom. He talked all the time, lightly, automatically, of parties generally, of army bottle-parties, of a particularly virulent drink in Italy (the name of which I forget) which leaves one unconscious for hours, and liable to behave with the utmost ferocity on awakening. He told a long, involved story about his own behaviour after a bottle of this stuff. He had apparently attacked a colonel and several sergeants, and regained sanity to discover himself being held down by six prostitutes, in a frilly bed. He was still clutching a handful of a woman's hair, he remembered. This I didn't believe.

After several hours the band made their first attempt at a tango, that most lascivious of dances. The coiling syncopated rhythm came slowly down the room with the eternal sexual insistence. 'Fiesta,' the name of the tune was, and it wound itself around the guests, even tired dancers in alcoves. Gradually the floor filled again with gently swaying, touching couples, moving in a ritual abandon. Garret danced a tango particularly well, as if he had grown up with the rhythm in his blood; translating it into steps was easy. But for once he was silent, as if speaking would break the mood so elaborately being built by violin and piano and muted saxophone. Doreen danced indolently by, winking slowly at me over her partner's shoulder. She looked somnolent and happy; Brendan had gracefully been abandoned; one man was as good as another, so long as he could dance and wasn't actually ugly. She passed in shining silver, her hair falling shining across young Moore's shoulder. Teddy danced by, this time with one of the Cronin girls, to whom he seemed to be paying passionate compliments. Her white prominent teeth were stripped for his regard, her eyes incredulous. At intervals, Mrs. Kiernan's great good-humoured, bawdy laugh shivered through the tango mood, like an unintelligible warning. Somewhere in the room she was happy; her party was working out according to plan.

Suddenly, as if the band was tantalised by its own rhythm, there was a pause, and then the innocent sugared strains of an old waltz came down the room, in ludicrous contrast with the tango. It was like walking over the borderline into another world—a graver, older, safer world of carefully muffled passions, and carefully muffled bodies. It was superficial and sweet and rather touching in its fragility, its vanished airs.

'God,' said Garret, 'I can't bear this—I never could bear old-time waltzes. Will you come down for a drink, Maeve?'

'I don't mind.'

We went across the cool, long hall, and down the couple of steps to the 'bar'—a small room which was always set aside for drink at parties. One of the workmen was acting barman. A couple of oldish men, the bald joking ex-boyfriends, were drinking whisky with Mr. Kiernan, whose eyes were bright with alcohol. He smiled vaguely at me and Garret:

'Nothing like it, nothing like it. Not a damn thing,' he said ambiguously, and we smiled at him, and said nothing.

Garret got a sherry for me, and a large whisky for himself.

'You've outlived orange squash, Maeve.'

'And you, port.'

'I've outlived a great deal more than port,' he said carelessly, letting another whisky rapidly follow the first.

'Cigarette?'

'No, thanks.'

'Neither do I—the resort of the feeble-minded. Shall we go up or shall I get you another sherry?'

'We'll go up,' I said, swallowing the last of the sherry.

There was a haze of heat and smoke and yellow light coming from the room when we got to the hall, and it was still Strauss, innocent and nostalgic. Máire and Brendan were sitting on a low couch near the chrysanthemums, holding hands loosely. They didn't notice us, and I suppressed the desire to break in on them.

'Must we go in?' said Garret. 'It looks good out there under the trees. The lanterns—'

'Yes, the lanterns. All right.'

'Do you need a wrap or anything?'

'No.'

We went down the steps. It was a dark, moonless night, utterly still. In a gap through the trees to the left the haycocks were darker blobs of shadow. The Chinese lanterns might have been poised delicately in the air.

The trees that supported them were lost in shadow. We walked along a small path leading to the orchard. The waltz followed us, sweet, insistent, unwinding its threads of outdated romance. Garret stopped at a white garden-seat, with a blue lantern swinging from a bush above it. He took out his handkerchief and wiped away any possible dust.

'It won't hurt your dress now, Maeve.'

I sat down, and he carefully lifted a fold of the green dress, rather than sit on it. Then he sat down beside me, directly under the lantern, and looked down at me with the strange, sated eyes.

'This seems very far away,' he said.

'From Italy?'

'From Dunkirk, from Narvik, from the whole bloody game.'

'I didn't know you were in Dunkirk?'

'I was. So was Tony Cronin. He is still.'

'I heard about Tony. I didn't know him very well—he was the boy with curly hair and the mouth-organ, who sat with you all the time at that party, wasn't he?'

'Yes. He was with me most places. He taught me everything I know. How to fish, how to shoot, even how to play the mouth-organ. And he taught me something else I've forgotten.'

'How to be happy?'

He glanced at me sharply through the habitual boredom. 'He was playing "Lily of the Lamplight" on his mouth-organ when his face was blown away. He was alive afterwards. His hands moved for a long time. They wouldn't let me put a bullet through him.' He stopped speaking, and I said nothing either. He played with the folds of the dress, watching them glisten like jade under the soft light.

'What the hell? ' he said then. 'He got out, didn't he? The bloody muddle he hated—English and Irish, who'd have preferred to kill each other, all killing Germans because that's what they were paid for doing. And Germans killing them for the same reason; smooth-faced, raw German boys who played the mouth-organ better than Tony. What's it all for, anyway? German girls are as good to sleep with as English girls or Irish, and doesn't it all end the same way, anyway? Bed somewhere and forgetfulness, whether you win or lose. What's the difference?'

76

'But that,' I said angrily, 'is death, mental death. If those are your ideas you're no better off than poor Tony.'

'I realise,' he said carelessly, 'that I'm a great deal worse off. But what does it matter?'

'You're not too old yet to acquire an intelligent attitude to life,' I said, ignoring his question. 'The war is largely a matter of conflicting ideals, and you and all the others are fighting for one of those ideals.' I see now how priggish it must have sounded.

'Ideals! ' laughed Garret. ' What politicians shout at each other across conference tables. What have ideals got to do with fellows being killed like flies on open beaches, and having their faces blown away?'

'Everything,' I said, 'else there wouldn't be any sense in it.'

'There isn't,' he said tiredly.

'Anyhow,' I said, 'if you don't believe in the fight for democracy intrinsically, why did you join the British Army? You aren't an Englishman. It can't have been patriotism.'

'It was something to do,' he said, bored. And quite suddenly he began to make love, with a conventional, tired air, a joyless search for something he would never find, because he had forgotten what it was. In how many ravaged cities of Europe had he dejectedly started the same search, I wondered? I made no attempt to snub his efforts at making love, however. One is always curious. Besides, there was Doreen's pact which it amused me to keep. Besides, I was sorry for him. I suddenly began thinking of what the war had meant to me. It had meant dark bread and no oranges, and my father and George Henderson shouting at each other across a room. It had meant little more. At school we had been on an island within an island; bombs and ravaged cities and mutilated bodies had never been able to penetrate. We had listened to war news as we would listen to a ghost story told around the fire. It was all unreal and shadowy and infinitely far away. What was real was the clang of the bell in school, the morning chorus of the Captain's hens and cock.

Only once before had I realised that war was a reality, and that was when France fell. The news had come one sunny morning during a lesson with Mademoiselle Grandet. Someone had shouted it to someone else in the corridor outside. Mademoiselle had paused, staring at a point on the far wall with dull middle-aged eyes. The colour had drained slowly from her cheeks, and before our astonished eyes, slow, hard tears were dropping on to the desk. There were a few titters, but from most of us a horrified silence. Fifteen-year-old girls are usually cruel and often merciless, but not in the face of vivid, intelligible suffering like this. And so we began to compare imaginary notes, and talk, until the pale, stunned face had again become aware of us.

I was not attentive during the rest of that class, because the fall of Paris had suddenly become charged with a personal loss. A warm breath blown by generations of romantics came to me, and I thought of the gay, wicked city whose life was stilled. I thought, second hand, of the little cafés, the bookstalls, the boulevards, the grey cathedrals, the daring, exotic sense of sin, the youth, the age of Paris. I had read *Trilby* and Moore's *Confessions of a Young Man*, and I had seen *La Bohème*; these had built up my picture, and ignited a dream of one day walking through the Latin Quarter, and the Rue des Crimes, and Montparnasse, and seeing ghosts of the shattered

Verlaine and Wilde around every street corner. And now I would never see Paris as she had been; not after two wars (or was it three?), since the time of the artists who had built my dream. But even that was only the shadow of a shadow thrown by the war. I was still apart from it, and almost totally ignorant of developments. And now it was still going on, and Tony Cronin had been killed, and Garret Hurley, who had been a laughing boy drinking port for a boast, had had his mind killed.

'I'm sorry,' said Garret. 'You are terribly bored. I always thought I could kiss agreeably. I've had enough practice, though perhaps with the wrong people. Would you care to teach me from scratch?'

'No,' I said, laughing slightly to cover up my gloom.

'I told you your mind was dead. It would be like kissing a corpse.'

'I assure you that you are mistaken,' he said, his eyes full of meaning. ' But you're bored,' he said again, with a change of tone.

'Not exactly,' I said, 'but shall we go in? We'll miss supper if we don't go, anyway.'

'All right,' he said indifferently. He doesn't mind, I thought. For one failure he probably has a dozen successes, if you could call it success. And suddenly, again, I was sorry for him.

'Don't you believe in anything, Garret? In God and heaven and hell?'

'I used to,' he said without interest. 'Now I don't know. There was a reason once why I believed. I've forgotten what it was. Something to do with plain chant. *Populi meus, quid feci tibi?* I was in the choir in school. It's all so long ago. What does it matter?'

I'd have liked to have said something to put him

right, but by this time I felt powerless before the wall of indifference, the ready, bored laugh. I said nothing, but I was unbearably depressed. When we came up the steps into the hall again, the lanterns were incredibly silly and childish. The music had stopped. Brendan and Máire looked as if they had not stirred; the slightly tilted heads, the hands loosely clasped. Just as we were crossing the hall, Mr. Cronin's plump, alcoholic voice came through from the drawing-room:

> *At the age of seventeen*
> *I was 'prenticed to a grocer,*
> *Not far from Stephen's Green*
> *Where Miss Henry used to go, Sir.*
> *'Twas there I fell in love*
> *With the maiden so bewitchin'*
> *And she invited me to*
> *A hooley in the kitchen.*
>   *Ri—toorla, loorla, la,*
>   *Ri—toorla, loorla, laddy. . . .*

Garret's eyes were fixed in inalterable irony as he glanced sideways at me, smiling with his lips. And just then Doreen came down the stairs, glittering, smiling, seeming to regard us from a higher plane of experience. Young Moore followed her, and we all stood together in the hall, waiting for the song to end before going up to the dining-room. After supper, I thought, the pattern will repeat itself: dancing, sitting-out, drinking. Somewhere, George Henderson, because of the last war, was pacing up and down a sleepless room, his eyes too tired to read any more. And somewhere miles away, a boy's bones lay hidden, the bones of a curly-haired boy who had played the mouthorgan at one of these parties. The same dawn would whiten over the burnt-out lanterns and crumpled dresses of this party, as over the crippled figure pacing his room, and the place (or places?) where the bones lay. It didn't make sense. We seemed to be dancing on the edge of a crumbling cliff. Everyone was laughing, and I laughed too, wondering at what. Doreen whispered: '*Nobody's* going to have to treat anyone else,' and we all went up to supper.

VIII

Diarmuid was to arrive at Amiens Street late on an October evening. I was there—he had written giving me the time of the train, and saying he had been carefully vague to his parents about the time of arrival. They were not there, and neither was the train. I waited on the platform with my back against a slot-machine, happy because I like railway stations and because Diarmuid was coming home. The war had not cast its shadow for very long, and I had put the unhappy realisation away with my evening dress the following day. I am like that, impressionable and superficial. Only two things have left indelible marks, my father's shadowy but very real patriotism (his image of the beautiful, wronged girl which had been with me since childhood) and one other thing which was to happen soon, but of which I was unaware on that evening in Amiens Street.

As I waited, I began to go over in my mind the stages of the journey: the trip by bus from Gweedore to Letterkenny, along a stretch of wild coast where the sea was a flickering indigo, changing colour with every whim of wind, and the land was rocky and barren and beautiful, haunted by legends of the Gaelic civilisation it cradled. If you looked back you saw Muckish Mountain coloured like a grape, and idly leaning, one shoulder higher than the other; and farther back there was Errigal, conical and purple and mystic, like a mountain in a dream. At Letterkenny—sprawling, friendly Letterkenny, indifferent to the Gothic beauty of its cathedral—you changed into a frightful train slightly worse than a goods train, which shattered body and mind until you got (miraculously) to Strabane. That piece of the journey was always hazy. You were aware that the last of Donegal was passing in beauty before your eyes, that you might never see it again, or you might never see it until you were old, and yet the effort of farewell concentration was too great for the shattered, lurching mind. And usually you missed the last enchanting glimpse of Errigal cut against the skyline, and spent the rest of the journey in despairing regret. Perhaps never, never again ... And at Strabane you got out, and walked into alien territory which was no more alien than the mountains of Donegal, and queued for permission to go through a part of your own country. And you thought angrily of the Great O'Neill, who had ruled this beautiful land like a king—he was a king in all but name. And you concentrated all your racial scorn and defiance into the glance you gave the unheeding, indifferent British official, who marked your case idly after examination. You thought despairingly how he had probably never heard of the O'Neill; was ignorantly, happily perpetuating an outrage.

The train you got into finally at Strabane was sheer luxury after the other one, like an armchair after a school bench. You were at peace and could watch the flying soft beauty of Tyrone, too soft after the austere magnificence of Donegal. There was rich pasture and there were well-tilled fields—it was strange seeing wheat after the perpetual oats of Donegal. The hills also were softer, more quietly blue—none of the beautifully harsh cobalt and indigo of the north-western mountains. Even the accents of the people who got in at Dungannon were softer, and nearly as attractive. They were not clipped, and their vowel sounds were beautifully long and rich—'long' became something like 'lowng,' a drawing-out of the vowel as if they loved it.

By the time you got to the Mourne Mountains it was nearly twilight (in late summer) and, anyhow, your mind was less responsive to the magic of the places after a day's travelling—the last time you were fully conscious was during the second Customs examination at Goraghwood—and you were only dimly aware of the Gap of the North, mysterious in half-light. But you came alive again at the flat familiar stretch of coast near Dundalk; soon it would be Drogheda, and then Dublin would be only an hour or so away. And there was that sense, nearing home, of a thread picked up again, and something laid away irrevocably in the past with other lost summers—another part of one's youth sealed for ever in the mountains of Donegal.

But a train was, by this time, rushing into the station, and Diarmuid was home. But he wasn't—it was only the train from Belfast, and I walked back to my slot-machine and stood watching the excitement of arrivals. People coming off the train had always had for me an exaggerated air of importance, an air of drama. It was as if they had first walked out of the wings, and on to the stage for a brief vitally important moment, and then gone back into the wings again. They fascinated me, these people I would never see again, and had never seen before. Where had they come from? Where were they going? Why should their lives have touched mine for just this moment? Take that young girl in the red beret, running towards the woman:

'I never thought yi'd be able to get away, Cathleen! You're a wee angel. Peter got it, and he says to tell ye ... '

Or that man with the grey face and tweeds touching the dreamy-looking boy, who was waiting for him, on the shoulder: 'Any change in her, Bobby? I rang twice from Belfast, and it was engaged. That's what I thought—does Tom know yet? Better say nothing; time enough for him to know when ... ' Who was she? What was wrong with her? While I stood wondering someone touched my shoulder, and there was Diarmuid, tanned, freckled, his yellow hair bleached white in front from the sun, smiling with the uneven white teeth.

'Maeve!' he said, eyes darker than ever under the bleached hair.

'But that's the Belfast train!'

'Ours was just behind. Look, Maeve, back there. You were dreaming.'

'I wasn't. I was eavesdropping. Oh, Diarmuid—I'm glad, glad.'

'So am I,' he said, covering my hand with the remembered soft fingers. 'Writing every day wasn't the same, was it?'

'It helped,' I said.

We walked arm in arm down the platform, and he left his case at the parcels' office—for the night, he said. He didn't want to be bothered with it. I watched his tanned, narrow fingers, turning over the palmful of small coins, and selecting one to pay for the ticket. The ordinary gesture, unnoticed in anyone else, took on a grave and lovely significance, like a movement in a ballet. It was a ridiculous idea, and would have been laughed down by Diarmuid if I told him, but I never did, and the lovely movement continued to delight me. I had almost forgotten it during the holidays.

'Now that's done,' said Diarmuid, slipping the ticket

into his breast pocket, 'we're going to eat somewhere. But let's just walk a bit first—I've got to get acquainted with Dublin again, bless her.'

'Aren't you tired, though?'

'Very tired of being alone so long,' and he pulled my arm through his, and slotted his fingers through mine. Laughing, we went down the long flight of steps into Amiens Street, friendly in neoned dusk. He began telling me about Donegal—he had the trick of making you see a place in about three words—and we walked along close to the high station wall, and into Beresford Place, with the Custom House lifting fluent white lines up against the dark sky. A cloudy moon showed for an instant against the dome, and we stood to watch it, and then, when it disappeared, we crossed Butt Bridge and stood again to look up along that enchanted nocturnal stretch of the Liffey.

'Dublin,' said Diarmuid, and we watched the streetlamps blowing in long yellow curls across the dark water, and a pair of swans, just below, arched lovely necks to the light. Farther up the river, near O'Connell Bridge, neon signs lay red and green and yellow on the water like a coloured garment gathered about Anna's shoulders.

'Anna Livia Plurabelle,' we both said together, and laughed, walking on up Burgh Quay, and talking suddenly of James Joyce, whose *Dubliners* and *Portrait of the Artist as a Young Man* we had read together. But we could never get *Ulysses*, and all we'd read of *Finnegan's Wake* was a few passages copied out in handwriting by the friend of a boy Diarmuid knew. At O'Connell Bridge it began to rain, soft autumn rain that spun itself like a web over the city and made yellow blurs of the streetlamps threaded along O'Connell Street. A light wind brought ghosts of leaves on to the pavement, after their soft vagrant flight through the dusk. Diarmuid caught a leaf between his fingers and put it unaccountably in his pocket. We ran for the small café which, long ago, we had adopted. Our clothes were clinging wet to us when we sat down in the friendly steaming little place, at last. Toni, the owner, smiled with endless white teeth from the corner, and his great Latin brown eyes rested sentimentally on us for a while before he came over.

'The holidays are over?' he said, beaming.

'Yes. For good this time,' smiled Diarmuid.

'We grow up,' said Toni, sighing, and the smile dropped theatrically and comically from his face.

'Just as well,' said Diarmuid, 'because it sometimes means you can order more than plain fruit drinks. Tonight we'll have coffee and chips and things. You know.'

'I know,' said Toni, 'a grill?'

'Yes,' Diarmuid said; 'two grills. Uncle Peter,' he went on, when Toni had gone smiling away, 'gave me a quid when I was leaving. I'd nothing but my return ticket and sevenpence. Not even enough for fruit drinks,' he grinned.

'He'd nearly trust us,' I said.

'Nearly. But I think Toni only looks sentimental. Though I believe his father often gave suppers to penniless young men. Joyce used to come here in his student days and he once left an envelope with something written on the back, under one of the tables. The old man was evidently a bit of a character, and he kept the envelope. He showed it once to Dad after *Dubliners* came out.' Diarmuid paused. He often did this at a vital point in a story.

'What was on it?' I said.

'A queer phrase,' Diarmuid said. 'Just this: "in a flaw of softness softly was blown." '

'I wonder did he use it anywhere?' I said.

'Not in anything we've read, anyhow. Perhaps, *Ulysses*'

'But if he wrote it here when he was a student, that was *years* before *Ulysses*,' I said.

'I know,' said Diarmuid, 'but you'd never know how long a man like Joyce would keep a thing before using it. Remember he took ten years to write *A Portrait of the Artist*.'

We were silent for a moment, each thinking of the spectacled, brooding, solitary youth sitting over coffee in perhaps this corner where we were now. Diarmuid spun a cruet with thoughtful, long fingers, and his face, with the slightly hollowed cheeks, was suddenly remote. And then Toni was beside us, with a clatter of crockery. He laid the meal before us deftly, and the coffee-pot in front of me, and was gone with an indulgent smile. I poured the coffee without speaking. I was utterly happy, as I had been in the summer with my face buried in heather on Howth Head.

'In a flaw of softness softly was blown,' said Diarmuid, 'that steam rising up from the coffee. Or smoke coming from a chimney on a very still day. Couldn't it be, Maeve?'

'Yes,' I agreed. 'Or misty rain like to-night. Maybe some day we'll find out.'

'Maybe,' he said, smiling in a sudden brief flash across the table, and holding my wrist when I offered him the cup.

'Take it or it will spill. Quickly, Diarmuid.'

'Sorry, Maeve. I was thinking that time, of something

I was thinking of all the time in Donegal. Us. We're old enough to marry now. Couldn't we, Maeve?'

'Now?' I said. It had never struck me.

'As soon as you can. It's silly waiting three years more. Our minds were made up long ago.'

'I know,' I said, thinking hard.

'We'd have to live in our place until I finish off, of course, Maeve. It's big enough,' he added, looking up, worried, spinning the cruet again.

'I know it is, it's not that. But it wouldn't work, Diarmuid. You know it wouldn't. We'd want to be on our own, and besides—'

Besides? There were so many things. There was the renewed feeling, born of sun and sand on a summer's day, that life was a flower opening in the hollow of my hand. I was not sure what I wanted to do with it, or what I was capable of doing. Somewhere Diarmuid fitted in (it was impossible to imagine life without him), but not now. Marrying now would be like taking a shortcut to a lake, and missing the beauty of the mountain road. It would be like draining a glass before savouring the first sip. Even then, sitting opposite Diarmuid, I saw how vague and illogical the images were. But I saw also, with certainty, that marriage was unwise if nothing else, at the moment. He was eighteen and so was I. But for the next three or four years he would be studying, and in the middle of a very self-contained social life. He would mature, and that might mean he would change. Pride and common sense demanded that he should be free during that time, and choose freely at the end.

'Besides?' Diarmuid prompted, leaving his fork poised, and steadily holding my glance.

'You'll be studying,' I said lamely.

'I don't see what that has to do with it, Maeve.'

'Would you have asked me if I had been going on, too?'

'I don't know,' he said honestly, his eyes still on my face. 'We'd have been together. But when I got that letter saying you wouldn't, I suddenly realised that things weren't as simple as they ought to be. I want you, Maeve. I want there to be no complications.'

'There won't be. I want you, too. But you'll have to graduate first. I'd be an interruption.'

'You would be,' he agreed, the dark eyes laughing. 'I'm sorry, Maeve, for asking you to share dependence on my people. They wouldn't mind, and although it wouldn't be what we want, it wouldn't last for ever. I only asked you because, well, there are dangers for people as alike as we are.

'On holidays,' he said, and the fingers joined around the cruet, 'I made love to a girl who worked very hard all night to make me, God help her sense and her taste. It was at a hop I went to with one of the men on the farm. She asked me to come for a walk down by the river. She had fuzzy hair and thick legs. I couldn't say no. I'm weak as hell with women, partly because I can't bear to insult them. And I hadn't the courage not to behave as she expected me to, though it would have been just as pleasant to embrace a sack of potatoes, and kiss a cabbage. If she had expected me to proceed further (which she didn't) I wouldn't have known how to refuse. Do you see?'

'Yes,' I said, 'I see.' I was thinking of the party.

'Go on, tell me yours. As true as God those aren't the eyes of an innocent woman.'

'That party I was telling you about,' I said.

'I knew it,' he said, unexpectedly throwing back his head in that quick glitter of a laugh. His throat, coming from the blue open shirt, was brown as a nut. No part of his face was untouched by the sun. Small freckles, the same colour as his hair, dappled the fair skin. Looking at his laughing, untouched youth, and placing it beside the remembered, jaded satiety of Garret Hurley, I grew abstracted.

'Wake up, woman. Is it as pleasant as all that to remember?'

'No,' I said. 'It was awful. He was at the war, and he didn't believe in anything anymore. He brought the war very close.'

'I know,' said Diarmuid, a shadow on his face. 'There was a fellow in Donegal too. A neighbour of Uncle Peter's. He'll never see again. He's twenty-two.' We were silent a moment, until the silence was broken by the ludicrous hiss of ice-cream soda. The shadow passed from Diarmuid's eyes and he looked up in sudden radiance.

'It can't touch us, Maeve,' he said, gay in the selfishness of the young. 'We might be in another world.' We were. We were not even part of Dublin on the rainy October night. My world had the four corners of the table for boundaries, on which Diarmuid leaned laughing across. And suddenly, looking at him, I realised what I was pushing into the future, always hazardous.

I was pushing away a climax of such terrible sweetness that the senses shuddered, thinking of it. Up to this, desire had been so easily satisfied, a hand clasp, the slightest contact. But now that a definite time-barrier had been raised, I was conscious for the first time of the despairing sting of the flesh.

'It isn't going to be easy, Maeve,' Diarmuid said quietly, thought reading not for the first time.

'No.'

'Is your mind made up?'

'Yes.'

'Then there isn't anything I can do but wait, and work like hell,' he said, lifting my hand and laying it against his cheek. 'I was afraid you wouldn't,' he added, smiling slightly over the hand.

'You agree it's better?'

'You can hardly expect me to agree. I accept it.' As he spoke, I looked up into his muted radiance, and I can still see the faintly hollowed cheeks (so beautiful in the tracing), the lowered eyes.

'It won't be long,' I said, full of despair, and his answer was a slight clouded smile from lifted eyes. We listened to the rain softly falling outside, through the 'Joyce country.'

Part Two

HALF IN DREAM

For the look out of any pair of eyes is maybe more than half in dream.

Brinsley MacNamara

I

Late in that year, just after Christmas, George J Henderson came in one night and announced in his diffident way that he had found me a job as librarian in a small town in Tipperary—that is, if I would like it. If I would like it! He was astonished, I think, when I squeezed his two arms and stared in incredulous delight into his face. It was as if he had offered me the world casually in his open hand. Disengaging himself gently, he blinked at me from the gaunt face, and explained that he knew a man called Monson who had several small lending libraries in Dublin, and wanted an enthusiastic young woman to take charge of a new centre in Tipperary. He had accepted George's recommendation of me. This seemed so far from the office job I had dismally hinted at to Diarmuid, that for several moments it seemed too wonderful to be true. I was to start at three pounds ten a week and end somewhere around six pounds.

The family was, on the whole, glad, although my mother stared at me strangely from fixed dark eyes before saying anything. I was to be the first of the family to break away, and I don't suppose it can have been pleasant for her. But in a moment she blinked the sadness from her eyes and began to give a most amusing impression of my telling the country people what to read. She was brilliant at this sort of thing, caricaturing me with brows, eyes, and voice. George laughed in real amusement, and so did Brendan and Sheila. Sheila had been doing home-work at the table, and it was now discarded. But when I looked across at my father, the fierce red brows were drawn together in a frown, and there were tears in his eyes. More quick-tempered than Mother, he was also more readily emotional than she was, and, anyhow, I think I was his favourite. Suddenly Mother's brilliant clowning was cut short by a loud wail from Bobby, who had been playing with coloured bricks on the hearth rug, and she flung herself across the room and buried her head sobbing in my lap. Presently she lifted a small face shining with tears, and fastening the wet black eyes on my face, she shouted passionately:

'Don't go, Maeve! Don't go! You're not to go!'

I was fond of the child, but even she couldn't dim my delight, even my father's sorrow. I dried Bobby's face, and took her on my knee, and sixpence soon quieted her. It was all I had, but what did that matter now? It is strange, but I can't remember feeling the slightest sorrow at leaving my home for the unknown surroundings ahead. Somehow the singing sense of excitement at the prospect of creating a life for myself was stronger than any regret at having outlived the old life, the old perfect security of my childhood. The prospect of change had always fascinated me. Even family holidays to dull little coastal towns like Skerries had always been shot through for me with the suffocating vivid excitement of the unknown. That was why I could look tearless at my father's tears, and at the quick shadow of pain in my mother's eyes. Their sorrow never touched me, nor did anything but rebound against the shining hard shell of my delight. Sunk in the hollow of the old couch, I thought that now, on my own, I should have a chance of realizing the vague dreams whose sting had prevented my marrying Diarmuid. I should be free to find myself—whatever that might mean. I saw the small southern town rising desirably through a haze of dream, and I thought of Charles Kickham and the lost homes of Tipperary.

The only person who made any real objection to my going away was Diarmuid, who made what almost amounted to a scene when I told him. I couldn't at all understand his attitude. He knew I had to get some sort of job, and it was foolish of him to have taken it for granted that the job would be in Dublin. Most people, after all, had to leave their homes, and some their country. I tried to laugh him out of the black mood, but it was no good, and of all the assembled eyes that I looked back into at Kingsbridge, as the train drew out of the station, it is Diarmuid's I remember most clearly. They were fixed on my face in a medley of expressions: anger, despair, sorrow, surprise. But his lips were smiling, the lopsided, unforgettable smile I loved, and his hair shone yellow under a lamp. Just as the train was moving off, he raced on an impulse after my carriage, and pressed my hand so tightly with the thin fingers that they hurt. He raced along, laughing, and keeping pace with the train until the end of the platform, and then stood watching in the cold January air, his hair wild. I stayed for a long time at the open window, smiling unconsciously into the darkness, straining for the slightest pale speck that might be Diarmuid, but there was nothing except the long chain of city lights strung across the darkness. He was gone. They were all gone and I was alone. I moved away from the window, full of a pulsing joy. Diarmuid's strange eyes, if they had been the last memory of him, might have clouded the mood, but they were not the last memory. I closed my eyes, and looked again at his long racing legs keeping pace with the train, at the forgiving radiance of the upturned face, and felt again the curving soft fingers covering mine. I opened my eyes, and glanced curiously down at my own hands. There was nothing to cloud the excitement of this journey through darkness into the heart of Munster, and into complete freedom. Somebody brushed suddenly past me in a mist of peppermint and slammed down the window. I looked doubtfully up into the angry face of an old gentleman in black, with a white scarf and white hair like cotton-wool floating on his head. He glared down at me before resuming his seat beside me and retiring behind the evening paper.

But I didn't care. He was old and draughts perhaps worried him. Besides, he saw no young face laughing in the frame of the window. He was old. Almost smugly, I considered this for a while, and then felt a foolish twist of pity for him, before taking up again the dropped threads of the reverie. It pleased me to think of the naked sleeping fields of flat Kildare, through which we were passing, fields bound by winter. But somewhere underneath the cold darkness, daffodils were pushing to passionate birth, a million green things were spearing the layers of heavy earth, pressing further and further into the light. In another month it would be spring—for me it was spring already. Everything pushes through the dark clay of its birth, I thought, and that's what I have done. It was *not* dark, I knew, and not in any way restrictive, but it was too solid, too secure. It was right that I should, for a while, break loose from every soft shackle, and breathe wild air of my own choosing. I was going to build for myself in that little town a shining bridge to the day when Diarmuid would qualify, and then everything ever afterwards would be built by both of us. But until then, life was mine, and it was sweet. I wouldn't have wished it otherwise, I thought in utter dilated complacency. I opened the book on my lap, idly, and read:

'Eyes, opening from the darkness of desire, eyes that dimmed the breaking east. What was their languid grace but the softness of chambering? And what was their shimmer but the shimmer of the scum that mantled the cesspool of the court of a slobbering Stuart.'

The book fell, as often before, and sleepily the phrase coiled: Eyes, opening from the darkness of desire, eyes that dimmed the breaking east. Softly the rhythm of the engine, churning the darkness, took up the lines, and beat them softly back into my brain. Eyes, opening from the darkness of desire ... opening from the darkness ... of desire ... The rhythm of the engine broke and slackened, and we were drawing languidly into Ballybrophy, and a yellow lantern blinked over the gloom of an empty waiting room. The old gentleman, sorry for his angry glare, touched my arm and offered a belated evening paper, calling me 'my dear.' I took the peace offering and smiled, and he immediately began giving me his impressions of Hitler, in a frail ticking voice that reminded me of the Mistress of Studies in school. It was Hitler for all the rest of the journey and I regretted the loss of my lulling, softly sensual mood. But he was really a nice old gentleman, with revolutionary views totally out of keeping with his age. We discovered we were getting out at the same station, and despite his fragility he courteously helped me out of the train, and handed out my case before seeing to his own. Standing with him on the platform, as the train moved lumbering on to Limerick, I felt suddenly and desperately alone, for the first time. Everything that was familiar and comforting seemed to pass away with the last swaying lighted carriage, the carriage which my family and Diarmuid had watched passing out of Kingsbridge. Perhaps they had felt then what I was feeling now. I had an insane desire to clutch on to the old gentleman's arm and say:

'Don't go yet.' But he was already buttoning up his coat and gathering his things together. Just then a small, cheerful, red-headed child charged on to the platform and bumped to a standstill at my elbow. 'Miss Walsh says to show you the way, miss,' he said breathlessly, taking my hand in a businesslike way and picking up my case with the other hand.

'Wouldn't you be Miss Cusack, miss, that's coming down to hand out the books? ' he said then, in a slightly doubtful voice, laying down the case again. He probably doubted my ability to hand out anything.

'Yes,' I assured him, suddenly getting back all my confidence at the sight of his plain, cheerful face and homely hair. 'We'll be going on, then, so,' he said, gently pushing me forward, and I said goodbye to the old gentleman, who was adjusting his white scarf.

'Have a peppermint, my dear,' he said, 'before you go, and you have one too, sonny. Wonderful thing for a bitter night like this, you know. I shall probably see you at the library,' he called after me, unwinding the scarf and tying it again more securely. We called goodbye and went down the steps into the hard, glittering January night. The road seemed to be mostly downhill (in the morning I discovered the town was in a hollow), and far back at the other end of Main Street there was a dark curve of hill with the ruined outlines of an old church blotting out the stars. It was a night of stars, hard and bright and moonless, and utterly still. The town seemed asleep. The only light was around a pub called Tilson's, where a few men pulled at pipes and made a soft southern blur of talk. They stopped talking as we passed and the pipes were suspended.

'Good night to you, Miss Cusack, and welcome,' came a voice from the crowd, and astonished, I said: ' Thanks very much. Good night.'

'Timmy Meagher, that is,' the small redhead informed me, 'that works above for Mr. Harrington.' 'Oh, I see. But how does he know me?'

'Sure, everyone knows about you, miss, and who else would be coming this hour of the night?'

I happened to glance at the lighted window of one of the houses we were passing, and from the curve of a curtain a pair of female eyes looked into mine, and then disappeared. It was a small town all right. But somehow the voice from the group of pipe-smokers had made it all seem unexpectedly friendly.

'Does Miss Walsh keep anyone else?' I asked.

'The schoolmaster until he left,' the child said. 'A proper aul' divil too, miss. We've a new one coming in a short while, and they do say he'll be staying with Miss Walsh, too, miss. Answer him better stay wherever he is, if he's anything the like of the last one.'

'He might be nice, though.'

'Divil a nice, miss, an' he a schoolmaster.'

'What's your name?' I said.

'Paddy Joe Duggan, miss, and we're nearly there. The last house there forninst you, with the woman hanging out the door.'

We had turned a corner opposite the church, and had turned into a narrow cobbled street, with small houses that seemed to be leaning their roofs together gossiping over our heads. Several curtains parted as we passed, revealing brief glimpses of eyes in candlelight.

'Wondering they were, what you'd look like,' explained Paddy Joe ingenuously, throwing a look up sideways at me from the big eyes which reminded me of Máire Lavin's. We were almost at the end of the street by now, and the form of the waiting woman assumed monstrous proportions in width. She gloomed through the narrow opening, outlined in light, and when we were within a few yards of her, she started (as if seeing us for the first time) and came out into the street.

'Wisha you're welcome, girl dear,' she said, wringing my hand, and then pulling the case from Paddy Joe. 'Get away home, you,' she said to him, pushing him off, and I had to run back a bit after him.

'Good night, Paddy Joe, and thanks,' I said, putting a shilling into his small hand. 'Is she cross?' I whispered.

'Thanks, miss, sure the pigeons wouldn't go near her roof,' he whispered back. 'Only she won't be with the likes of you,' he said consolingly, and then ran off soft-footed down the street. I walked back uncertainly to the house into which Miss Walsh had already vanished.

'You must be kilt with the journey,' she said, meeting me in the hall. In the light of the oil lamp in her hand I had a good look at her. She was a great, flat, sprawling woman in loose clothes, the colour of snuff, and smelling not unlike it. Her face was big, and incredibly wrinkled, the colour of a walnut, and her mouth was shrunken from the loss of all her teeth. But her eyes were richly brown, almost beautiful.

'I'm not so much tired as cold,' I said, realising suddenly that it was true.

"'Tis a thief of a night,' she agreed, 'and you after coming the whole long way from Dublin.'

I followed her into the kitchen, through the tiny hall with its looped red curtains smelling of dust. The kitchen was much more rustic than I was prepared to find it. The oil lamp, set in the middle of the deal table, showed a low-ceilinged, smoky room with a big open fire and a bewildering array of objects tumbled all over the place. A mattress was rolled up and standing in one corner, and a bundle of clothes ready for washing was thrown in another. At least six leering china dogs were ranged along the mantelpiece, three on either side of an alarm clock, indicating the time as two-thirty. Lace curtains on the one window were not falling from the rod in the ordinary way, but the end of each had been caught up, so that it appeared as if each side of the window had half a curtain. Three geranium pots (empty) were standing under the window. I looked in some alarm for some sign of a staircase, and there, in a shadowed corner, was a twisted flight of steps, narrow as the width of an arm, leading up to unknown dark regions. The place smelled of dust and turf and oil and—surely?—cats. Yes. In front of the fire on a 'creepy' stool there was a gigantic shining black cat who turned steady, brilliant green eyes in my direction and slightly twitched his stiff glossy black whiskers. Miss Walsh pushed me briskly into the only chair in the room, which was drawn to the fire. She moved with amazing agility for such a huge heavy person. I stretched out my hands to the flames, leaping in rich colours, and felt for a moment as if I were another person, washed clean of every memory of every other place.

'It's a lovely fire,' I said.

'And wouldn't you need it on a night the like of this?' she said, eyeing me expertly all over from tossed hair to numbed fingers. Her tone softened.

'It'll not be long before that kettle is singing, and then we'll have something will warm the cockles of your heart. 'Twill put new life into you, girl,' she ended, as if she thought I badly needed it.

'That will be grand,' I said, wondering when she would put the cat off the stool and sit down. Finally I got tired waiting, and tired of the feeling of being examined from a great height.

'Won't you sit down, Miss Walsh?' I said.

'Wisha, I'd liefer stand, and, anyhow, that creepy is Peter's. 'Tis often I have to stand when a body comes in for a chat. Peter of the jewel eyes I call him, and wouldn't they put you in mind of two jewels, the eyes of him?'

'They're beautiful,' I said, wondering when Peter, too, would stop staring.

'That lad is the father of half the cats in this town,' Miss Walsh said proudly. 'A walking divil. Isn't that right, Peter?' Peter lifted his head at his name and gave an affirmative flash of the jewel eyes. He was a beautiful cat; I was not surprised at his success.

'Peter's great-great-grandfather,' continued Miss Walsh, 'came to this town with me forty years ago since Christmas. Mind you, 'tis a queer town enough— we're still strangers you might say. I was born in the city myself.'

'Were you? In Dublin?'

''Deed no, in the city of Cork. I was seventeen years of age when the mother died on me and I went to an aunt in the city of Waterford, God be good to her. A cancer put an end to her, the creature. I came then to a brother of mine that lived here in this house, God be good to him. He died two years ago, and here I am ever since. Yerra 'tis lonely enough, and you with not even an aul' schoolmaster to sit by the fire of an evening. People comes and people goes—the like of Mossy Derrane the fiddler and travelling man, but sure that might be only twice in the year, and maybe once. 'Twill be a change to have a young girl the like of you around the place, and maybe the new schoolmaster, if God is good. Is it in Dublin you'd be born?'

I recognised this as a signal for me to begin my autobiography. Her own was simply a polite introduction to mine. So, knowing there was no help for it, I began, telling her details of my origin and family and describing, at her request, the house, the locality, the type of neighbours, and anything else she thought of asking me. She thought of plenty, and her astonishing lively brown eyes shone in the brown face at the profusion of my information. She visibly warmed to me, and when the kettle bubbled in front of us, she took away one of the two mugs on the table and replaced it by a blue china cup from the dresser. Reticence, I fancy, would have resulted in my drinking from the mug. She made tea in a chubby, earthen pot, and spread yellow butter thickly on the oaten cake. The tea was good, and the butter was unheard of luxury to someone coming from rationed Dublin. I discovered she was an amusing woman, with a flair for gossip, and also a priest-worshipper. Poor Father Tom began to take up an increasing amount of the conversation, and I grew weary of his perfections, and also sleepy. This she noticed after some time and cut short an account of the previous Sunday's sermon to remark:

"Tis time you were between the blankets, Miss Cusack dear, and the eyes closing in your head this minute.'

Relieved, I got to my feet, and out of the direct radius of the fire the air was sharply cold. I shivered, and envied Peter his bed in the ashes. But Miss Walsh was already, candle in hand, preceding me up the stairs, and I followed her, suddenly losing all desire for sleep. The candle flame cast her monstrous shadow on the wall, and I, unused to candles except at Kiernan's, thought it gave an air of sudden evil to the place. I wished there had been somebody else there, or even that Peter had decided to follow us upstairs. But Peter was probably lost in warm dreams at that moment. We crossed a minute square of landing full of trunks and picture frames and tumbled clothes, and she stopped in front of a dusty, narrow door. There were two doors.

'I'm putting you in the big room, Miss Cusack,' she said, 'and if himself decides to stay here when he comes, like the master before him, sure we'll let him do with the weeshy bit of a room off mine.'

'I'm sure he won't mind,' I said, and then realised that this was perhaps not the most discreet thing I could have said. But she didn't appear to mind. She flung open the door, which immediately banged off the end of the iron bed. Peeping over her shoulder as she held up the candle, I saw why. The room was the size perhaps of a large coffin. The bed took up the whole length of it, and along the near wall there was barely enough room for a narrow chest-of-drawers affair, with a jug and basin on top and a small cloudy mirror, the size of a tea-plate, slightly higher on the wall. I was appalled, not so much by the size of the room as by the size of the window, which securely sealed off all air. The place reeked of the dust of generations. Thick layers of dust lay along the frames of the bewildering array of religious pictures covering every inch of the walls, except the very few inches taken up by the mirror.

'You'll be as snug as a bug in a rug in here,' said Miss Walsh. 'Every bit of heat from the kitchen comes up. I put your bag under the bed there, but sure your things could stay there till the morning. May God give you a good night's rest,' she said, giving me the candle.

'Thanks very much, Miss Walsh,' I said. 'Good night.'

As soon as the door shut behind her I stepped across and wrenched at the small window. But it might have been merely decorative for all the good it did me to pull at it. How long ago it was since anyone had opened it—had anyone ever opened it? Despairingly I tugged, imagining that every breath I took was poisoned, which perhaps it was. But it was no good. And then I had an idea. I tore the things out of my case until I unearthed my hairbrush, which was strong and big because of the thickness of my hair. Grasping this, I brought it down heavily on the top ledge of the window frame, and it slammed down suddenly with a crash. A whiff of beautiful icy wind blew into my face, and there was a dazzle of frosty starlight. The stars had been dim through the coated glass, but now they made the twisting flame of the candle look pallid and spent. Anxiously I waited for the sound of Miss Walsh's angry feet up the stairs—surely the crash must have wakened up the street?—but there was no sound except the lonely howl of a dog, and the love-call of a cat. Gratefully I hung out through the window in the pure frozen air, and looked along the length of the cobbled, starlit street. It was beautiful, with its softly shadowed rows of small houses, each with a pointed porch, and the gracefully tapered Gothic lines of the church rising whitely at the far end. A cat streaked dark across the cobbles, sprang with perfect restrained grace at a low roof, and disappeared over the top. I thought of the conical high Galtees flinging back reflected lights to the stars, somewhere here in the darkness, not far away. I thought of the unknown sleeping people very near, whom shortly I should know. And as I leaned out in the cold air a sharp sense of excitement caught me by the throat, and I felt like singing. But I didn't sing. I jerked back into the room and decided immediately I was going to make it mine. I began by making a clearance of the worst of the pictures—sleeping with them all around me on the walls was unthinkable—and soon a dusty pile of blue hideous Madonnas and outrageously coloured Divine Persons and saints was before me on the floor. I pushed them all under the bed, leaving only the austere classic beauty of Our Lady of Perpetual Succour on the far wall, and an El Greco Christ—how had that found its way here?—over the bed. Would Miss Walsh understand that all those horrible things were not 'religion'? In the reckless mood of that night, the questions did not worry me very much, as I placed George Henderson's beautiful model of the Customs House (the only thing from home I'd brought) on top of the chest-of-drawers, nearest the window. Tomorrow I would clean up the room, since Miss Walsh obviously did not consider any cleaning necessary, and then it would be all right. Happily squatting on the bed, I picked up the book I'd been reading on the train, and then in horror I remembered I hadn't looked at the bedclothes. Suppose when I turned back the sheet to get in I saw crawling little horrors moving down the bed into safety, waiting for darkness to attach themselves to me? I went cold at the thought, and fearfully peeled down the clothes inch by inch with one hand, and held the candle down close with the other. But the linen was amazingly fresh and spotless and smelled of moth-balls. Even so, once the idea had got into my head, I examined the blankets, the inside of the pillow, and the mattress, and even under the mattress. They were all impeccably clean and I could laugh at myself.

I did laugh at myself later when I was between the sheets and looking up at the walls naked in candlelight. They were not my walls. What right had I? But I regretted none of the hideous pictures, and happily stretched out an arm for the book. I might be in Tipperary, but when I touched Joyce I touched all Dublin, all home. With no nostalgia, but only a lazy peace, I read:

> *A veiled sunlight lit up faintly the grey sheet of water where the river was embayed. In the distance along the course of the slow-flowing Liffey, slender masts flecked the sky, and more distant still, the dim fabric of the city lay prone in haze …*

Lulled by the slow, lovely languor of the prose, and turned towards dream by the picture, my eyes closed, and I was almost asleep when I stretched for the candle and, without opening my eyes, blew it into darkness.

II

Thin winter sunlight lay pale on the walls when I wakened the following morning. It was only seven o'clock. I'd always wakened early. I lay there listening to the cheerful cackling of the hens (were they Miss Walsh's?) and the persistent conceited shrilling of a cock. It was almost like home, only the Captain's cock was louder and more arrogant. Possibly he had more hens at his disposal. What had I been dreaming of? It had been strange, but I couldn't remember. The hens had splintered the last fragments of the dream. All I remembered was Diarmuid's face, vaguely floating near mine, and the wind tearing his yellow hair. He had been trying to tell me something, shouting above the wind, but a girl's fingers had closed over his mouth. Yes, that was it. But where were we, and who was the girl? It was no good, I couldn't remember. Perhaps I should dream it again. I sprang out of bed into air razor-sharp with frost, but beautifully fresh. Mr. Monson was meeting me at the hotel at ten o'clock, to get me started at the library, but I couldn't wait till ten to look around the town. Besides, I wasn't sleepy, and the prospect of a walk before breakfast was attractive. On holidays in a strange place, I'd always gone out on the first morning, and this was like a holiday in so far as it was a complete change. I imagined my mother's comments on the primitive sanitary facilities, but I had always been adaptable myself. It was wretched though, washing in cold water which had gathered a doubtful scum from the rims of the basin, but I expected I would get used to that too. Anyhow, my mother had insisted on putting a small bottle of disinfectant into my case—'You never know, with country people, Maeve'—and that would be useful for scouring. Mother regarded anyone born more than ten miles outside Dublin with the gravest suspicion.

While brushing my hair at the mirror I reflected that the virtue of humility would be easy to acquire here. The face which looked back at me appeared to be blemished by innumerable black spots, but on closer inspection these proved to be blemishes on the face of the mirror. Nevertheless, they were disconcerting enough to make me hurry, and in a few minutes I was opening the door softly, so as not to waken the possibly sleeping Miss Walsh. The precaution was unnecessary, because I heard feet below in the kitchen. At the sound of them, I took a swift look back around the ravaged walls of my room, and my nerve failed me. I remembered her bright eyes which could, I was sure, singe one in anger, and I remembered with a sinking heart Paddy Joe's whispered remark: 'Sure the pigeons wouldn't go near her roof, miss.' Without a moment's hesitation I stepped back into the room and proceeded to restore the horrible pictures to their places, working as swiftly as I had worked last night. The result sent me running rapidly downstairs, my coat half-on:

'Good morning, Miss Walsh.' She was pouring boiling water into an enamel jug, a vast stooping figure still in the snuff-colour of yesterday. A slender ray of sun touched the back of her neck. She sprang around with one of her quick, unexpected movements at my footsteps and voice.

"Wisha, what has you up this hour, girl? I was just going above this minute to give you your first call, and leave the water for you to wash yourself.'

'I always get up early, Miss Walsh, and I just thought I'd have a bit of a walk before breakfast. But I'm sorry I missed the hot water.'

'Small blame to you for that. It's a wonder the teeth aren't shaking in your head with the perishing cold.' 'It's not so bad really,' I said. 'Anyhow, I don't feel the cold much. I won't be long.'

The brown eyes stared in astonishment at me from the brown wrinkled face. Going out before breakfast on a frosty morning *was* crazy, of course. Peter, from the hearth, lazily opened two shining green slits and shut them again.

'Did you get a good night's sleep itself?' she asked, as I was going out through the door.

'Like a log,' I assured her, letting myself out into the sun.

A couple of women, blinking and sleepy, were hurrying along to the church, but both turned to look at me and call a greeting. This habit of people in the country and in small towns had always appealed to me, and seemed infinitely right and natural, the spontaneous acceptance of one human being by another. It was always one of the things I missed most after a holiday in the country. Even if the friendliness was allied to an insatiable curiosity—these eyes had watched through curtains last night—what of it? Wasn't curiosity natural too? Indifference was hostility. I walked on up the street, my breath making ephemeral patterns in the air, and suddenly the Mass bell sang out, climbing down sweet and shrill through the sunlight from the turreted belfry. I should go to Mass; half the town seemed to be going. And it would be a good beginning. But somehow I persuaded myself against it. I had always lacked the direct simple piety instinctive in most of the people I knew. I was a Catholic by upbringing and conviction, but Catholicism often irritated me, the outward signs of it, that is. I disliked the spectacle of people praying in public, the closed or upturned eyes, the beating of the breasts. I was never more remote, or less devout, than in the middle of a praying congregation. I was restless, bored, critical in an absurd way of the clumsy movements and ritual piety of my neighbours. So I walked on past the church, past the townspeople filing in and sprinkling holy water. For a moment I was conscious of the gulf between us, and wished I could span it.

I turned left at the corner, back up Main Street through which I had come last night, and passed Tilson's, deserted now in daylight. Farther on there were a few small drapers' shops, another pub called Danagher's, and in a small clearing surrounded by green railings, there was the new schoolhouse, cream-washed and fresh-looking, waiting for the new schoolmaster. Up at the station there was the noise of the first train from Limerick rushing through, and a sooty cloud widened across the pure icy skyline. I crossed the street to the dingy, dark-red Royal Hotel, in front of which there was a memorial to the young townsmen killed in action during the fight for independence. I stood for a while looking up into the stone face of the young Volunteer who looked for ever over the butt of his rifle into the dark hotel lounge.

> *In proud and grateful memory of Michael Danagher, Joseph Meagher, Patrick Ryan, and Kevin James Lonergan, all of Tipperary, who were killed in action against enemy forces in April 1919.*
>
> *Do chum glóire Dé agus onóra na h-Éireann*[2]

---

2   For the glory of God and the honour of Ireland.

Passing back down the street towards the church again, I could see them, Michael (a young brother of Danagher the publican, perhaps?), Joseph, Patrick, and Kevin James, normal, laughing young men on the edge of their fives, suddenly forsaking everything for the illicit gun, and following the red flare of a dream to their deaths. God knows who struck the spark that came to flame in them; some young ancestor with a pike and an ideal, who had been crushed in '98, but whose dream had not died? The smoke of centuries of burnings and oppression, the smoke of Charles Kickham's lost homes of Tipperary, had risen between these young men and their normal lives, and they had lost all desire for everything except to follow in the dead footsteps, and to take up the weapons dropped from dead fingers. The shawl had fallen back again from the immortal face, and they had looked into the young eyes. And they had hidden in their hearts the flame out of the eyes of Cathleen, the Daughter of Houlihán. The Young Girl who had broken through the poetry of the dark eighteenth and nineteenth centuries, and had broken four times through the life of them, had appeared again in the twentieth century, and nothing would ever be the same again. Not even now, so long afterwards, and with the ideal partially realised. Always, in somnolent little towns all over Ireland, there would be the ghosts of those young men, hovering over memorials in market squares, stinging one into remembrance that the dream was still a dream, shattering complacency.

Suddenly I realised that during all this idle reverie I had left the streets behind and was climbing the steep rocky road up to the hill which, last night, had risen against the stars. The ruined church was gapped and naked in sunlight, with the black arms of a winter tree stretching up through the shell of a belfry. Cromwell was perhaps the last to see this church as it had been. Perhaps he had looked into the hollow of the town, as I was looking now, and searched for something else worthy of his torch. But my glance moved left, far out beyond the roof-tops and farther than the red-brown winter fields to where, in the distance, was Slievenaman, the fairy mountain. It rose in a soft, soaring curve, deeply blue, as if winter had never touched it, and it were showing through the haze of an enchanted summer. Slievenaman, the mountain which had bloomed through a thousand folksongs and stories. And moving in a circle past it, the eye touched the bright slopes of the Knockmealdown Mountains, to the south, and nearer home, very close in fact, the speared, sharp beauty of the Galtees. My picture of them last night had probably been accurate, because this morning their peaks were frozen to a dazzling whiteness, and their lower slopes, wooded, softened to black velvet. Startled, I saw that it was already nine o'clock, and I had to see Mr. Monson at ten. What would Miss Walsh say? I ran back down the road, which shone with dangerous brilliance in the sun.

'You know that stone memorial down in front of the hotel, Miss Walsh?' I said to her during breakfast. 'Did you know those boys?'

'Know them? Why wouldn't I, and they born and reared here? They got into trouble with guns, the poor unfortunate lads, and got kilt. Young Danagher was a brother of Con Danagher that owns the public house down there. Sure, they had no better sense. Answer them better go and earn their living like everyone else and never mind going agen the English. Weren't we better off under the English, anyway?'

'Were we?'

'Sure, of course we were, and lashings of money coming into the country, and plenty of work going for them that wanted it up at the big houses. What more did we want? The freedom of Ireland, God help us—a lot of poetry-talk like you'd hear out of Mossy Derrane and his likes. No matter who's ruling the country, don't you and me have to go about our work in the same way?—only there's less money to be got out of it now. Eat up that egg now, girl, that's only fresh from the hen. Mass it was that kept you, I suppose?'

'No, I didn't go to Mass. I went for a walk up on the hill.'

'A walk up on the hill and Father Tom saying the holy Mass not half a mile away! God forgive you, Miss Cusack. Wait till Father Tom hears that.'

'Were you at Mass, Miss Walsh?' I thought I had her here.

'Six o'clock Mass every morning of me life, Miss Cusack, and Father Tom himself will tell you that.' 'I'm sure he would if I asked him. You're wonderful. I'll have to be going now, Miss Walsh, it's almost ten. The ends of your curtains got caught up,' I said, because the sloppy look of the looped lace was irritating.

'Yerra, not at all, girl. I do keep them like that to keep the ends clean. Sure, they'd be black in no time if you let them hang. Will you be in for your dinner? ' 'Not to-day. Mr. Monson wants me to have a meal with him at the hotel. Good-bye, Miss Walsh.'

'You'd want to have a care what you'd eat in them places,' she said contemptuously. 'Good-bye now, Miss Cusack, and a safe journey to you.'

The hotel was two-minutes' walk away.

III

I had only met Mr. Monson once before, in Dublin, and he struck me as a rather amusing little man, full of shy importance at the fact of his being president of the Dublin Amateur Writers' Group. This fact, George Henderson said, coloured his choice of lists for the libraries, and he purchased a lot of 'bloody tripe' which seldom got further than the shelves. George's idea of bloody tripe was the plays of Tchehov and the works of Guy de Maupassant, François Mauriac, and other continental writers. Mr. Monson had impressed on me, at our first meeting, that the people of County Tipperary were exceptionally literary, and when a reader asked for advice there was to be no question of recommending Peter Cheyney. What Ireland needed was a firm understanding hand to build up her taste in literature, and there was a tremendous scope for this in the provinces, which had so long been neglected. He knew, from experience, how responsive the people were to intelligent guidance. His small libraries (mostly run in conjunction with local shops) in Adare and Athenry and up in Carrigart were doing exceptionally well. He had every reason to believe that the centre in the small town in South Tipperary would do well also.

I found him waiting for me in the dark hall of the Royal Hotel, under a couple of branching antlers. He was dressed, as I had seen him before, in a peppery tweed jacket vented in two places at the back, dark brown corduroy trousers held up by a crios[3] and he had a yellow knitted pullover. He might have been a rather gay university student, except for the sleek white hair and anxious middle-aged face. His blue eyes had a rather pathetic expression, very anxious to please.

'How are you, Miss Cusack? How are the digs?' There was a touch of Dublin in his voice.

'I'm fine, thanks, Mr. Monson. The digs are—well, I suppose they will be all right.' He looked extremely worried, and rumpled his hair with a small hand.

'They assured me Miss Walsh's was the best place for a girl to stay,' he said, not very clearly. 'They said the food would be excellent, and that Miss Walsh was a kind woman.'

'So she is,' I agreed, 'very—except to small boys. The only thing is—' I stopped. How could one begin to describe the disorder of the place, the size of the bedroom? I decided not to try. Mr. Monson looked worried enough. 'I expect it's just that I'm not used to digs yet,' I said, 'but it won't be long before I am. She has plenty of butter,' I ended cheerfully.

'That's grand,' he said, greatly relieved. 'She might fatten you up a bit, wha?' Dublin broke irrepressibly through the acquired gentility.

'I doubt it, Mr. Monson. As an old nun we had in school used to say, "what's bred in the bone." My mother, after five children even, is still as thin as I am.'

'Em,—yes,' said Mr. Monson, playing with one gold cuff link. 'Would you have a drink with me, Miss Cusack, before we go down to the library?'

'Not now, thanks, but I will at lunch. I've just swallowed breakfast. And I'm dying to have a look at the library, anyway, and get started.'

---

3   Belt or girdle.

'Good, good. We'll go at once.'

'But don't you want a drink yourself?'

'No, no, not at all,' he said vaguely, and we went down the steps together. His manner was in outrageous contrast to his clothes, and his taste in books. But I liked him. He seemed an ideal employer, and he was the first person I'd ever met who seemed slightly afraid of me. That was pleasant.

We walked down Main Street and took a turn to the left around by the church. The bank was here, and the local dance hall, and a very new, very wildly coloured cinema called the Scala. Mr. Monson talked more freely as we went along, telling me about George Henderson in the old days when they played tennis together. George had been brilliant and was famous for his speed, and his unbeatable, highly individual service. He was also the best dancer in the club, and was competed for by the prettiest girls at club dances. Mr. Monson was not exactly a good talker, but he had a certain vague, evocative power in his voice, which gave you the feel of those remote, lost, Edwardian summers, innocent of so much which was to happen so soon.

The library was part of a sweet-and-stationery shop called Harding's. The bookshelves were at the back of the shop, and well-lit by a long, wide window on the far wall. Mrs. Harding was to look after all the financial end of the business; Mr. Monson and she had come to an arrangement. My job was wholly concerned with the books, issuing them, date-stamping them, writing membership cards, keeping the books in condition, and sending on selected lists of requested additions. But this last was with reservations. I must attempt to develop the taste of Tipperary along the right lines.

'You and Mrs. Harding will get along famous,' said Mr. Monson, hopefully and very nervously, as he introduced us. She was a dour, small-eyed woman of fifty or sixty, who looked at me insultingly, as if she thought I were at least twenty years too young to get along with anybody. She said almost nothing in a slow Tipperary voice for about two minutes, and then left us abruptly to provide a small boy with bullseyes. Mr. Monson looked timidly at her implacable face over the counter, and then led me down among the books. He opened a briefcase and produced a neat typewritten catalogue. I glanced down the lists, amazed at the standard of the books.

'You see the sort of books we go in for, Miss Cusack?' he said, with a small inflection of pride in his voice.

'Yes,' I said slowly. 'It's a wonderful list, but if you don't mind my saying so, I shouldn't think the people here—'

'You're quite wrong, Miss Cusack, I assure you. Did you ever read Lady Gregory's book on *Our Irish Theatre*?'

'No,' I said, feeling guilty at the omission.

'I suppose we can't read everything, isn't that right? But if you had, Miss Cusack, you'd've been struck by her wonderful, calm insistence when she says: "We kept on giving them the best until they began to like it." Just that, and those few words hold her whole spirit and her whole ideal, don't you know. Long ago I adopted them as mine too. I kept on giving them the best until some of them, at least, have begun to like it. Do you understand?' he ended, turning up the anxious, uninspiring blue eyes into my face.

'Yes, and I'm all in favour. It's just that I thought a library like yours wouldn't make money.'

'Money?' said Mr. Monson, dreamily. 'Oh no.

It doesn't make money in the real meaning of the word. But it doesn't lose very much, after the first few months. As you'll see, the books are mainly ancient or modern classics. I *have* got a small sprinkling of popular novelists. They draw people,' he said sadly, and fingered the dangling fringes of his beautiful, vivid crios. He showed me the record-system, which was very simple, and explained the usual routine in the most apologetic, soft voice. Then he left me, after repeating (in varying degrees of humility) an invitation to lunch with him. I spent most of that morning happily idling among the books, discovering several that I had wanted to read. One of these was Graham Greene's The Lawless Roads, and I finally took that up with me to the desk, and started on the strange prologue, so touched by despair. It seemed very far from me and my excited anticipation, and I liked the contrast, as one likes listening to a storm from the refuge of bed.

A few times I was disturbed by the noisy clearance of Mrs. Harding's throat, and once or twice I caught her small eyes fixed challengingly on me. When I smiled at her, she noisily lifted a box off the counter and replaced it in the same position.

IV

The first day proved to be misleadingly slack, because very soon afterwards people began to get interested. I was kept busy writing membership cards, which cost two shillings a year. The member could then borrow books at the rate of twopence per book per week. I kept the membership money and charges per book in two different boxes, and there my part in the financial end of things ended. I was glad of that because handling money had never been my strong point. I'd never been able to make even my small private accounts make sense. Mrs. Harding, on the other hand, handled money with the affection and skill of a lover. Her small bony hands moved unerringly through the coins at the end of the day, and then flicked through my record slips. When she found they tallied, she would strip her small sly eyes at me and brush one palm lightly against the other. She never spoke, except to make some unintelligible sound to my peaceable 'Good morning.' Once I saw her laugh. A small boy had left back one of the 'William' books on my desk, and for some reason she picked it up and opened it. After a while her face cracked across in a laugh, but when she caught sight of my astonished face the smile went out like a match, and she hurried back to her counter, with one of the familiar hostile glances at me. For a while after that I was toying with the idea of offering her the book to read, but I hadn't the nerve.

Sometimes I was amazed by the choice of books made by some of the members. Mr. Monson had not been so far wrong. There was one woman in particular I noticed, a slattern who would come in with her hair bristling with curling pins, and always wearing slippers. In a voice like Limerick butter she would ask for Boswell's *Johnson,* or Blake's *Collected Poems,* and once for de Maupassant's *Bel Ami.* Her taste was catholic in the extreme. I tried a few times to talk to her, but was repulsed. One of the most faithful readers of detective fiction was the old gentleman on the train, who evinced not the slightest interest in the handsome volume of *Mein Kampf* on the shelves.

I had been in the town for about a week when Brian Clancy, the schoolmaster, came. On Sunday, at Mass, poor Father Tom announced the imminence of the master's arrival to his assembled flock. Poor Father Tom had a habit of making important little speeches about nothing at all, as I afterwards discovered. He was a small, eager man, with a perfectly bald, oval skull, and a striking blue intensity in his eyes. His mouth was small and curved and clever looking, but actually I don't think he was intelligent. He was perpetually preaching about the beauty and necessity of early Christian marriages, and was perpetually patrolling the lanes at night to scare home dallying couples. His voice was terrifying because of the size of him. It rolled out rich and full from his narrow mouth, and one sometimes got the impression that if it went one note higher his whole frame would be shattered. That Sunday he stood in front of all the uplifted faces, and leaned slightly on small claw-hands over the dusty plush of the pulpit. A finger of light touched the end of his nose and grazed one eye, making it brilliant.

'To-day, my dear brethren, I have a most important announcement to make. We have had, as you all know, and as you all regret with me, to prolong the Christmas holidays because we lacked, through the thoughtlessness and inconsideration of a young man—because we lacked, I say, a schoolmaster. I have now, with some difficulty, procured another young man, and I wish you to welcome him in your midst in a manner befitting a person with such an important calling. There can be few such important callings in the world to-day as the education of youth. In youth are set the seeds which will take flower, for good or evil, in after life. In youth are set the seeds …'

The rich full voice overflowed from the plush pulpit out over the heads of the flock, and with interest I watched the faces, stained here and there with coloured sun through the windows. I could see Miss Walsh's worshipping, uplifted profile, absorbing every word, like a man who drinks after a long thirst, with the prospect of a longer one. I could see several faces I had often seen at the library, only now they were all vague in concentration. Congregations, such as this one, and a voice such as Father Tom's, have always reacted on me like quiet music, and I remember closing my eyes, conscious of nothing but the last sentence moving slowly through my brain: 'In youth are set the seeds.' That voice was one of the seeds, all the assembled faces another, the small town, deserted now in winter sunlight, was another. All these were the result of my choice, for all these I had swopped the remembered joys of Dublin, and what would I get in return? But gradually, as so often before, all the questions and idle thoughts dissolved themselves into one face, and the image widened until it covered all my brain, and I was conscious of nothing else. Diarmuid déad geal, dreach-sholuis, Ó'Dhuibhne. Somewhere in Dublin, the frosty sun that came through these windows was lying on his hair, and somewhere, in some city church perhaps, his face was turned up in abstraction to a spot on the ceiling, and he was composing the letter which to-morrow would slip through on to Miss Walsh's dusty mat. Think. Minds can touch sometimes with the intensity of concentration. Think. The sun on his yellow hair, the yellow sun on his yellow hair, and underneath, the unexpected darkness of the eyes, and the faint hollowed cheeks, and the vulnerable mouth that could break, in a moment, into the wonderful young smile. But he is not smiling now. Think. The delicate unquiet fingers playing with the leaves of his missal, sliding along the smooth leather cover. Suddenly Father Tom shouted me into awareness of the church and the sermon, and I blinked up into his little angry face—what was he angry about?—and I thought: 'The next time I go to confession I'll have to say again: Father, I was deliberately distracted in church. Father, I committed sins against the ninth commandment. Father, I … ' but once again I drifted out of the congregation and into a shimmering country where Father Tom could never follow.

And so, that afternoon, when Miss Walsh was bustling around the house, taking things out of places and putting them back again, I couldn't understand why. Usually, she just sat half sleeping in front of the fire, coming alive occasionally to ask me questions.

'Are you expecting somebody, Miss Walsh?' I asked her. I was trying to concentrate on a book. It was a cold day, with a naked strip of sky showing coldly through the window. Often my mind would stray from the book and out to the sky, as it had done during the morning's sermon.

'Wisha, girl, where's your head at all, you that's supposed to be bright? Did you not know Mr. Clancy the new master was coming here to-night? He'll be beyond teaching school to-morrow morning.'

'Oh, I see.'

'And why wouldn't you? Wasn't poor Father Tom near kilt this morning telling us the way we should put a welcome on the same Mr. Clancy, and he so hard to get and all?'

'Do you know him?'

'Divil a know I know, only that he comes from the County Kerry. It was God sent him these hard times. Mightn't it just as easy have been some young lad from around, that would be after leaving the college and that would go and stay with his own people. There's Paddy Kiely and Tom Maher up at the college these years, but sure what class is the likes of them to be teaching school, anyway?' Miss Walsh swiped a cloth across the table, and dared me with her bright eyes to disagree. I contented myself with saying:

'Where will you put him?'

'Where else only in the little bit of a room that runs at the back of me own room. If I *do* go up some nights before him itself, sure what harm will it do him to pass through and I in me bed?'

'No harm,' I agreed.

'Sure, divil a harm, and he a Kerry-man that won't have much of the green boy about him, I'm thinking.'

'Do you think would Father Tom like it?' I said soberly, looking innocently at her.

'Divil take that Peter! ' she said in alarm. ' Will you look at him at them chickens again.' She rushed out and I didn't see her again until it was nearly dark, and I was crouched at the window with my book, catching the last flakes of daylight.

The prospect of the new schoolmaster staying in the house was interesting, because really I had had very little company since coming. The people in the town were friendly, but not anxious to pursue the friendship further than a few remarks and several questions while they were waiting for me to stamp a book. So far nobody had asked me to go anywhere. On evenings when it wasn't fine enough to follow the road up the hill out of the town, I just sat in with a book. It wasn't very easy to read by candlelight. But just about this time I was beginning to feel that the adventure was wearing a little thin. I loved the work at the library, and the borrowers were a source of unfailing interest to me, but I was beginning to realise why people rush away from small towns on any pretext. There was very little to do—except one liked the highly coloured films which the local cinema favoured. I didn't. Also, around this time, I was beginning to get nostalgic for Dublin and everyone there. Sometimes, when alone, I would close my eyes and let my fingers run along the arms of a chair, delicately feeling what was not there. And the mood that would flow warmly over me was like water lapping naked limbs. One took so much for granted at home. His face on Sundays framed in the half-opened door, and his voice:

'I only looked in for a minute, on the way to the match. Would you never decide to come?'

'You know I hate soccer. I told you often enough.'

'Well ...' His strange dark eyes would be remote, straying over one's features as over a half-remembered country. He would take up one's hand almost absently and look at it, stroking it precisely with narrow fingers, curving at the tips. Silence. A car would go by. A child's screaming laugh down the street would do no more than graze the edges of abstraction.

'Well ... ' His eyes would suddenly stop wandering and lie still, peaceful in their darkness, as if something had been found. He would suddenly laugh. 'To-night, then?'

'To-night. Why did you come?' But I would know. 'I was just passing. I knew you wouldn't come to the match—you said so yesterday. But I knew you'd open the door when I knocked—you always do—and so ... ' The young, wonderful smile. The light fingers, still playing with mine.

'You'll be late, Diarmuid.'

'Yes.' He would smile again, the smile so blatantly contradicting the dark early maturity of his eyes. ' Good-bye.' But saying it, he would still stand there, as if he had forgotten where he was going. Yes, in Dublin one took so much for granted.

It was late when the knock came to the door, and Miss Walsh sprang to open it with her usual amazing agility. I amused myself at the fire by wondering what he would be like, this Brian Clancy from Kerry. I could hear the voices at the door.

'Wisha, you're welcome, Mr. Clancy dear, and you after coming the whole long way from Kerry. You must be kilt entirely from the journey.' Just what she'd said to me. Not much could be gathered from the vague replies one makes to such a greeting, except that his voice was Kerry all right, lilting and very soft, with a certain quality in it that could be coaxing. A moment later he was in the room.

'Let you shake hands with Mr. Clancy, there, Miss Cusack dear, and put a welcome on him. Miss Cusack does be working down the town in the library, Mr. Clancy.'

'You fit the chimney corner fine,' said Mr. Clancy to me with the easy friendliness of his county, and he shook hands and sat down immediately on Peter's creepy stool (Peter had had an appointment to keep). Then he drew it closer to the fire, stretching his hands to the flames, and smiling up at us with his attractive, almond-coloured eyes, which held the firelight.

'You're welcome,' I said, eyeing him in some surprise.

'As the cuckoo,' added Miss Walsh. You could see she was going to dote on Mr. Clancy. Before he had realised what she was doing, she had disappeared up the dark stairs with his bags, quick as a porter. He turned to me and lifted one black eyebrow—I discovered afterwards this was a habit of his—and then he smiled, concealing for a moment the cleft in his chin, but revealing a set of perfect, shapely teeth. I noticed the three touches of white—eyes, teeth, collar—set against the soot-black, curly hair, which curled away slightly from the temples. Too good-looking to be interesting, I thought, wondering when I could politely depart to bed.

'Queer old hen,' said Mr. Clancy, in a loud stage whisper, 'isn't she?'

'Yes,' I agreed. 'She'll dote on you.'

'Why?'

'Quality,' I said. 'Mr. Clancy the schoolmaster that's staying with me—you know. I like her, though.'

'What's your name?' His hands were still cupping the flames.

'Cusack,' I said.

'I know—she told me that. What's your name?'

'Oh, Maeve.'

'Brian they call me,' he said, tilting a smile sideways from his eyes. 'Brains they used to call me at home in our place—in Rathmore.'

'Had they any reason?' I said.

'Well now, that requires consideration, don't you know,' he said, the lilt in his voice now very noticeable.

'Come to think of it … ' And he broke off as Miss Walsh swept into the kitchen.

'I'm after leaving your bags up in the room, Mr. Clancy dear, and sure you can take out your things any time at all. Tell me, would it be from the town of Tralee you'd come, now?'

'It would not,' he said, glancing into Miss Walsh's face with an amiable effrontery.

'Look at that for you now!' she said, her invariable remark when nonplussed. 'Fancy that now! I'd say from the voice of you it wouldn't be far away from there.'

'There was a man I met once, and he was English,' said Mr. Clancy, taking us both into his confidence with two brief glances sideways, 'and do you know what he said to me? "I'd know," said he, "a Galway accent anywhere, by Jove, what? Am I right, sir, what? " Is it any wonder now, the English would be losing in the war?'

'Sure, the Lord save us,' said Miss Walsh vaguely, looking down at the new lodger with a shadowy dissatisfaction on her brown, creased face.

'The English are terrors,' went on Mr. Clancy, with perfect composure.' I lived over there for a year once, and the silence drove me home again. When they aren't saying stupid things like that man, they're saying nothing at all, and sure you wouldn't know which was the worst. You could travel five hundred miles in a train and not hear two words spoken, only maybe what you'd say yourself.'

'Sure, the Lord save us!' said Miss Walsh again.
'Teaching I'd say you were over there, Mr. Clancy?'

'Indeed, I was not.' Mr. Clancy's laugh was rich and loud. 'I'd rather teach pigeons manners than try to teach the youth of England.'

'Look at that for you!' Miss Walsh's face was now frankly disappointed, and her large brown eyes were chastened in defeat. She said:

'Maybe, Mr. Clancy, you'd like to come up to see your room now? '

'Certainly, ma'am,' he said, winking slowly at me before following her up the stairs. He had the sort of wink that would, I thought, dispel sadness in a flash. I wondered what he would say to me about that room if Miss Walsh were not there.

Next day I found out. I was just going out to the library when he said, ' If you wait half a second, Maeve, I'll be along with you, girl.'

It took him more than half a second to knot the yellow-and-black scarf about his neck and get on his thick coat, but I waited. He banged the door loudly after him.

'Holy Mother of God,' he said, ''tis good to get the pure air into your lungs again. Take a deep breath, that's right. Do you know you'd nearly have to go out the door to put the shirt over your head, the ceiling is so low. And if you went out the door, 'tis in her room you'd find yourself, and you showing an unmannerly amount of your person. She's no right to be putting temptation in a man's way, has she?'

'Or in her own,' I said, laughing at him.

'Or in her own,' he agreed placidly, running a hand along his chin and then exploding in a rowdy laugh.

'A wonder,' he said then, 'she didn't think of putting yourself and myself so close.'

'Perhaps she did, and then thought again. Are you dreading your first morning in school?'

'In a way I am, Maeve. Children are unpredictable.'

'Well, good luck.'

"Tis how I'll need it,' he said, waving his hand in gay contradiction as I crossed the road. When I looked back there were two boys scuffling outside the school. One had snatched the other's cap. I wondered vaguely for a while how he would get on during the day, before my thoughts returned to circling around the question why there had been no letter from Diarmuid that morning.

V

A few days afterwards I got a letter from Máire. Máire wrote seldom to anyone, and her letters were always limping and short and affectionate. I read this one several times, and while I was reading it Brian Clancy took up the previous night's paper and appeared immersed in it.

> *Dear Maeve,*
> *I hope you are well and happy as I am. It's very cold here. I see Doreen sometimes, but not often. She doesn't go around much with us anymore. She likes College. I wish you hadn't gone away, Maeve. Last week I saw Doreen, and she was running away with Diarmuid's gloves through Stephen's Green, and he was running after her. A girl who lives next door to us is at college with Doreen, and she says Doreen's very excited about some dance she's going to. She has a new frock. I've been called to the Civil Service – 'Writers.'*
> *Brendan is a very nice boy. Sometimes he says to come into your house. Your father keeps joking, but he is very nice too. Last night I was there. They are all very well. There was a man there called George and he and your father were talking about the war. He is very nice too. I will now conclude, hoping to hear from you. I miss you. I am no good at telling things in a letter.*
> *Máire*

I could see her, crouched worried over the paper, biting chunks out of her pen as she always did in school. I could see the red long hair flopping on to the page as she wrote, and see the troubled indecision of the great innocent eyes, pondering the next word. She had not written for nothing. Neither had she written all she had intended.

A longing to be home caught me by the throat and I clenched my eyes shut until it had passed. 'I wish you hadn't gone away, Maeve.' The words danced mockingly through my brain and I remembered with despair Diarmuid's strange appeal not to go. What had I done? Why should I not have gone? The second question arose in immediate answer to the first. The whole thing was ridiculous. If the disturbing little picture of Doreen racing through the bare trees and filtered sun of the Green with Diarmuid after her had any meaning, it was not of any consequence. Why should he lead a hermit's life because I had chosen to go away? Half convinced, I dropped the letter on the table and turned again to my breakfast. The tea was cold anyway, and I pushed it away. That letter was heavy with untold things. And anyhow, why wasn't Diarmuid writing anymore?

'She drums fingers in the approved style on the table and stares ambiguously into the middle distance,' said Brian Clancy, tiring of the silence and looking across with one eyebrow lifted. I suddenly hated the happy good looks, the clear amber neutrality of his eyes.

'She stops staring ambiguously into the middle distance and stares instead with definite hostility into the face of one Brian Clancy, who is fretting to be off to his work, but who, nevertheless, desires to wait for the lady.' There was nothing but good humour and friendliness in his face, and as suddenly as I had hated him, I warmed to him. What was the sense in blaming him?

'I'm coming,' I said, trying to fight the flood of remorse and despair that swept over me again, as I got up from the table. Peter looked up from the hearth into a thin ray of sun coming through the looped curtains, and he reminded me of the cat I had seen that day outside the school railings. That day seemed to belong to another age.

Somehow, the day trailed to an end, and five o'clock found me out in the cold sun of Bank Street, unwilling to go back at once to the house. The thought of Miss Walsh's warm, cluttered kitchen, smelling of turf and dust, suddenly filled me with distaste. But Bank Street, swept clean by January winds and palely lit by January sun, was unobtrusively comforting, and I went slowly along, prolonging the stretch of sonorous cobbles. I would not go back just now. I turned up right through Main Street and on up the hill to the broken church. The light this afternoon was good, golden and clear and harsh, and the mountains would be clearly stencilled on the skyline.

'We could take that bit of a road up the hill and not be too late for tea,' a Kerry voice said, and there was Brian Clancy at my side, laughing, the sun showing yellow in his eyes. The fringes of his scarf were lightly lifted by the wind, making him look like a postcard undergraduate.

'Hello, Brian. I thought you'd be home long ago.'

'Two scoundrels that I was keeping in late,' he explained. 'It's the only thing they care anything about. You could leather them until the arms would fall out of your sockets, and damn the heed they'd pay to you. But keep them in hammering at Irish after the others and they'll think twice before coming in again without their irregular verbs known.'

'Irish verbs?' I said.

'Irish verbs, God help us. Though what good the same verbs are supposed to do an unfortunate little gossoon like Paddy Joe Duggan I won't presume to say. But it's my job to teach them, just the same, and it's what I'm mainly paid for.'

'And that's the only reason why you teach Irish?'

'Certainly. What other could anyone have?'

'There was a time once when people like you thought it worth their while to teach Irish for hours at night in stuffy little rooms in Dublin and teach it free, *and* teach it after their day's work.'

In impatience with Brian Clancy's lukewarm nationality I had lost the creeping melancholy of the day, and in the hope of an argument I was suddenly happy, feeling a cold exhilaration when the wind tore my hair back from my face.

'More fools they, girl. Flogging a dead language back to life is the work of a heedless idealist. It would do as much good to tell people go round swinging green cloaks after them and playing harps around the streets of the cities. Constructive fighting for the material freedom of the country—yes. All honour to the men that won it. But the idea that freedom is inseparable from the native gibberish is pure idiocy.'

'Then Pearse was an idiot, and so were all the men who won the material freedom you put such store by?'

'Connolly, who fought as well as any of them, didn't give a curse for the language.'

'But you insist that Pearse was an idiot?'

'That's putting it a deal too strong, girl. Pearse was a dreamer of dreams and no more to be examined logically than any other dreamer of less broad and less important dreams.'

'Editing a newspaper, running a school, and planning an insurrection down to the last detail, were odd pursuits for someone who was merely a dreamer.'

'No one but a dreamer could have done them all,' said Brian Clancy, acutely, 'but the point is, Pearse never brought his ideal of an Ireland not merely free, but Gaelic as well, not merely Gaelic but free as well, outside the realm of dream. He never had a chance—going down in the heat of the fight, as he did, he had never a chance to put the ideals into practice. If he had, if his sentence had been commuted as Éamon de Valera's was, he'd soon have thrown overboard an idea as impractical as the nationwide revival of Irish.'

'Éamon de Valera is an unfortunate choice, Brian. Has he thrown over the revival of Irish?'

'Not yet—he'll be forced to eventually. His pig-headedness has resulted in a country of unfortunate little ignoramuses—thrown out to earn their livings at fourteen, with not a word in their heads except a few pieces of gibberish which their first job is to forget as soon as they can.'

'That just isn't an accurate statement of fact—you're deliberately blind. I was at a national school myself until I was thirteen, and when I moved on to a secondary I was more advanced in every subject, not alone Irish, than children of the same age who had learned through the medium of English.'

'You must have been an exceptional child. Going by present indications, I'd say you were.'

'I wasn't. And I hadn't even an exceptional teacher—possibly she wasn't as exceptionally defeatist and passive as you are. Everybody who came out of that school—everyone with average intelligence—had a better grounding in everything than English-taught children. It came out afterwards in examinations.'

'Then what are the parents talking about? Pick up any local rag and the first thing you come across is an attack from "Pater Familias" on the evils of teaching through Irish. They say ordinary children taught through Irish and having to leave school at fourteen are totally ignorant.'

'And does the fact that they say so make it true? Teaching through the medium of Irish is a Government policy, and therefore it is attacked the same as any other Government policy.'

Brian Clancy sighed and flung a fringe of his scarf back over one shoulder. Then he smiled charmingly down into my face, light-filled golden eyes full of indifferent good-humour.

'I'm stubborn as a mule, Maeve,' he said. 'Nobody will ever convince me that there's any sense in working for the rebirth of a dead language *against* the will of the people—not even you.'

'A handful of enthusiasts have brought the work along so far. Another handful could complete it.'

'I can imagine you up on a soapbox among the trees of Stephen's Green, with the wind making bits of your hair, and the light that never was on sea or land blazing through the two eyes of you.'

The argument degenerated into flippancy, as arguments with Brian Clancy were wont to do. He was really a most irritating person, but irritation with him never lasted long. Before we got back that evening I was listening with much interest to his gaily expounded plan for forming a local dramatic society. At Miss Walsh's door he broke off talking about this suddenly, and tilted up my face to a streetlamp. Smiling, he examined it, until I wriggled free, and then he said:

'You look a deal merrier than you looked at post-time this morning. I wouldn't let it worry me, Maeve,' he ended quite seriously and very kindly. ' I waited for you on purpose at the corner, girl. I wanted to get you fighting.'

'I knew,' I lied, to take him down a peg. His eyes laughed at me, and we went in to tea.

VI

February came and it brought arctic weather and the first tentative stirrings of Brian's dramatic society. It also brought a few strange letters from Diarmuid, the nearest approach I had ever seen him make to conventional letters. That was what made them strange. He hoped I was very fit and enjoying smalltown life. For himself college company bored him slightly more than college lectures. Brendan and Máire Lavin were doing a strong line. Did I know? They were appearing everywhere together and ended up every night in the Ritz. Máire was becoming quite beautiful, but never saw anyone in the Ritz. She strayed in and out with the look of one who on honeydew has fed and drunk the milk of Paradise. Brendan was little better. Wouldn't I write some time I had time? There was nothing wrong with the letters—I only knew that they would not have been written a few months ago. Gradually I got used to them and could look back with contempt on the morning when life had seemed to be slipping perilously through my fingers. I was going up to Dublin for St. Patrick's Day, or rather catching a late train on the Eve, and then I should see for myself. Until then I decided to try to forget the whole thing, at least to push it so far back in my mind that it could not intrude against my will as it had been doing. Only sometimes, when I handled a book we had read together, when I passed it across the counter to someone for whom it had no associations, I would suddenly be caught in the grip of crowding remembered sensations, and I would be jolted back like a fitful sleeper who dreams he has missed a step in a long flight of stairs.

Brian Clancy was an antidote to all this. Almost every evening after tea he would jump up and reappear dressed for outdoors, holding my coat and scarf in his arms and asking if I knew I was going out. He had awakened a vast enthusiasm for the proposed dramatic society among the local boys and girls, and, most amazingly, in Father Tom also. I asked him how he had persuaded the priest to send around a plate at last Mass on three successive Sundays to defray the cost of erecting a small but adequate stage at the end of the big classroom, which with the addition of a few chairs could be used as a hall. He shrugged: "Twas child's play, girl. I told poor Father Tom that the first play we would do would be *Desire Under the Elms*, and sure there was no holding him back after that.'

Brian Clancy flung back his head and gave the rowdy laugh. He never showed his teeth much when talking, and the white brilliance of his smile always took people by surprise.

'What play did you tell him you'd do next? A dramatisation of your own of *Madame Bovary*?'

'True as God I never thought to tell him that,' said Brian, with regret, and I doubted if I would ever hear the true story. I never did. And for a while it puzzled me how a priest, notorious for chasing prospective lovers home through the lanes with the blackthorn stick, should condone a collection for erecting a stage, theatres (and substitute theatres) being traditionally associated in the pious mind with sexual immorality.

However, at one of the first meetings of the infant society I understood. Brian presided, seated up at his own desk in the schoolhouse, with groups of boys and girls, squatting on the tops of the pupils' desks, all around him. He carefully took off his scarf, laid it across a chair, then turned around to the company and lifted one even black eyebrow.

'To-night I want to decide finally on the play for our first production. I have an idea myself, but let's have your ideas first.'

There was, as is usual after an announcement of the sort, a long uneasy silence. There had never been a dramatic society, or any other society for that matter, except a praesidium of the Legion of Mary, in the town before, and so the members were still extremely reluctant to air their views. The very first meeting of all had been farcical. Brian Clancy had spoken for the whole length of it himself, amusingly and wittily and almost completely irrelevantly. He had ended by asking if there were any more speakers, and on receiving no reply, had declared the meeting closed. But the next time, the tension had not been nearly so great, and Peter McManus had spoken determinedly for half an hour on the plays of Agatha Christie. But the meetings still took quite a while to warm up, and while they were in the process of so doing, Brian and I took it in turns to speak about anything remotely connected with drama that occurred to us. At the last meeting I had given an abridged reading of Lady Gregory's *Our Irish Theatre*, about which Mr. Monson had made me curious. At the end, Michael Tilson, the publican's son, had actually been stirred into speaking. He rose to his feet slowly, his blushing, indignant cheeks a slightly deeper shade of red than his hair.

'I heard tell,' he said, 'that all the money that woman made out of the big the*ay*tre up in Dublin went for making Prodesdans out of little children.'

There followed a comparatively lively discussion on proselytizing after both Brian and I had exonerated Lady Gregory. Which fact took nothing from the liveliness of the discussion, or the repeated slandering of the lady. Brian, however, was not unduly put out about this.

'I don't give a tinker's curse what they talk about so long as they talk. If they can't be got to talk, how in God's name are we ever going to get them to act? '

So now, even at the third meeting, there was a long pause after Brian had issued his invitation. A few people were whispering together; Michael Tilson, with head tilted, was rapidly making notes on the back of an envelope, his feet comfortably planted on the bench in front of him, and his knees in the hollow of Bridie McMahon's back. Bridie, a merry-eyed girl with a red beret, did not appear to mind. Brian coughed and looked appealingly at me, after raising his eyes to the ceiling for a brief moment.

'I suggest,' I said, 'that we do something worthwhile, as well as easy to stage. How about *The Playboy of the Western World*? ' The meeting immediately came alive. I knew it would.

'I think it would be asking for trouble to put on a play the like of that in this town,' said Michael Tilson, jumping to his feet and thrusting his red, bulldog face forward. He was liberally freckled, and his stiff, wavy, red hair sprouted upwards on his head.

'What class of a play would it be, now?' Bridie McMahon asked, with rapid interest. 'I heard tell of it all right, but that's about all.'

"'Tis a bad class of a play,' Michael Tilson said decisively, looking to the chair for support. 'Am I right, Mr. Clancy?'

'Well now,' said Brian, darting a quick delighted look at me, 'I don't know so much about that. It depends on what you mean by a bad play.'

'You know fine what I mean, Mr. Clancy,' and the publican's son flattened the stiff brush for an instant on his head before the hairs sprang up again under his fingers. 'Women standing up in their shifts, and bad language and drinking, and all class of carry on.'

'Sure, wouldn't that be a bit of a laugh? ' said Bridie, with a giggle, looking flirtatiously across at the indignant Michael, with her merry eyes.

'The Dublin people didn't think so,' Michael said darkly, ' when they near riz the roof of the theaytre the night the play was acted.'

'Janey!' said Bridie, taking us all into her round glance, 'we'd maybe have Father Tom roaring down on the top of us. That stick does put the heart crossways in me,' she said. This last remark to Peter McManus, a clerk from the bank, who was beside her, with an arm loosely round her waist. They subsided into whispers, and a plump, rosy girl, with her lips illicitly and inexpertly rouged (she was from the Holy Faith Convent, five miles away, but lived just across the road), stood up and said:

'Why don't we do *Night Must Fall*? It's a spiffing play, and I know who'd be a lovely Danny.' She blinked up at Brian, and drew in a deep, deep breath. It was common property in the town that she was a member because of an infatuation for the schoolmaster. Her name was Maureen Walsh and her father owned the Royal Hotel. Brian smiled charmingly down at her and cleared his throat.

'You've made a few very good suggestions, those of you who spoke, but for our first production I think it must be Shakespeare.'

'Shakespeare!' exploded half a dozen voices. 'For God's sake, Mr. Clancy!'

Brian lifted a hand, and his voice had an easy, mellow assurance about it. 'Listen to me. The fact that our first production is Shakespeare doesn't mean we're not ever going to do anything but Shakespeare.' He paused, spun a pencil between his fingers, and with a couple of brief, bright glances around the room, gathered everyone's attention. 'Tell me, do you think it was for *Night Must Fall* or its likes that Father Tom sent around the plate for three Sundays?' There was a quick burst of laughter as with a droop of the shoulders and an intense, brilliant glare from the almond eyes, Brian Clancy, for a moment, was Father Tom. 'Yerra, not at all. What he wants (and I don't know but he's right) is to increase the cultural activities of this town, and to give the people an appreciation of good drama. You're not going to tell me that he's pushed whether the people appreciate Night Must Fall or not, are you? Even you down there, Maureen?' Maureen dropped her glance and fingered her hair, and then gazed up again with mouth slightly open at the speaker.

'No,' said Brian decisively. 'Whether we like it or not, it will have to be Shakespeare, and maybe Agatha Christie would get a look in some other time, herself and Mr. Emlyn Williams. How about *The Merchant of Venice*?' It took not a great deal of persuasion to fix on *The Merchant*, because everyone could see that Brian had made up his mind, anyhow. I was glad, on the whole, about the choice. It had always seemed to me one of the sunlit plays, with Shylock as the first, faint shadow that would deepen into the tragedies. It recalled a long summer term in school when we had studied it—I could still feel the heavy, hot, clinging of black wool to legs that ached for sunlight, still see the delicate powder-puff clouds poised in hot air outside the classroom window, still hear the soft, tired voice of an old nun reading the glorious passage of young Portia's surrender:

> *You see me, Lord Bassanio, where I stand,*
> *Such as I am ...*

Brian and I were tidying up the classroom after the meeting was over when there was a tap on the door, and wondering, I opened it. In the half-light of the narrow passage Maureen Walsh was standing, a finger on her reddened, heavy lips. The light from the classroom showed her short, chunky body, and red face, empty even of the vivacity that makes all young faces transiently beautiful. She handed me a scrap of paper rolled to a soft ball.

'Give it to him,' she whispered. 'Will you?'

'All right, Maureen.' She hesitated, smiled blankly at me, and walked away uncertainly. I imagined her standing in the shadows by the wall outside, isolated in difficult adolescence, watching the flirting laughing boys and girls disappearing in groups down the street, listening for the sound of Brian's footsteps, regretting already the crumpled ball in my hand.

'Who was that at the door?' Brian called across the room. He was moving a desk back into place and was rather out of breath.

'Maureen Walsh,' I said, coming over to him.

'God give her sense,' he said. 'Show me what she gave you?'

'Who told you she gave me anything?'

'Don't I get them every other day, girl? Sometimes she gives them to the boys for me, and for that again, she'll throw them through the window.' I offered him the ball of paper and he caught the hand that held it and squeezed. His hand was warm and firm and its pressure was not unpleasant. When I looked up I looked directly into the warm, golden friendliness of his eyes, brighter now with a need brought on by the silence of the little schoolhouse, and the darkness lying against the window panes, and the passivity of my hand lying in his. There was a soft thud of falling ash in the grate, and suddenly I wanted him to kiss me, in a vague, absurd desire to betray Diarmuid. The bitterness and fear of the past few weeks flashed past my mind, and I lifted my face smiling. With a quick translation of the thought Brian pulled me closer, and touching his mouth I felt that I was touching everything normal and healthy and human, everything opposed to the shadowy misery of my thoughts recently. I was cut off in a happy syncope, where nothing existed but a warm, comely, human body so close to mine that I imagined I could breathe for both of us.

'Hello, Maeve,' he said presently.

'Hello, Brian,' I said, tracing the outline of his face with the fingers of one hand. The memory it brought made me turn away, miserable, disenchanted.

'You've been unhappy, Maeve,' he said, still holding on to one of my hands and gently pressing it with his forefinger.

'Yes.'

' If I can ever be of any use—'

'I know.' He squeezed my hand tighter in perfect, ready friendliness, and then unwound the paper ball with a laugh to which I knew he wanted me to respond.

'Poor little Duckling,' he said, with nothing of mockery in his voice. Without showing me the paper he dropped it into the reluctant ashes, where it lay unconsumed until we were at the door and Brian had just clicked off the light. Then with a small sound the paper sprang into flame, lighting up the black bars of the grate. I thought of the child huddling outside in the shadows.

VII

We were ready to go down to the schoolhouse on the night before I left for Dublin when we heard a voice out in the hall, a rich loud voice that was full of the West. In a moment Miss Walsh was in the room, followed by a magnificent brown-skinned giant of a man gripping a violin under one arm, who seemed at once to fill the kitchen. He had the eye of a king—wild, brilliant, arrogantly blue—and a tawny growth of beard. The wretched tattered clothes might have made anyone else insignificant; they were merely a foil for his powerful body.

'Dia dhíobh,'[4] he said, coming over to the fire, and looking piercingly through the wild eyes at Brian and me.

'Dia is Muire dhuit,'[5] we said together, and the giant laid his fiddle on the hearth and sat down, stretching out great brown shapely hands to the blaze.

'That's Mossy Derrane for ye,' said Miss Walsh, proudly. 'He never passes through the town without stepping in here.'

'And why not, I ask you?' said the fiddler, ' when you put a welcome fit for a king before me.'

'There's not so much of your breed left now,' said Miss Walsh, with a smile at him, 'that we would turn you away. Indeed there's not.'

---
4   *God be with you.*
5   *God and Mary be with you.*

'Are you from Galway?' said Brian, sitting down on his heels in front of the fire and flinging away his scarf over the table. The big man looked at me, when I squatted down too, and then he rose to his feet regally.

'Be seated there, a chailín,'[6] he said to me, 'and forgive an old man for the manners he's forgotten.' I thanked him and took the chair, not daring to refuse, and he stood up tall in front of the flames and drew the gaily coloured wool belt tighter around his waist, before sweeping the contemptuous Peter off his stool with one movement of a huge hand, and saying to Miss Walsh:

'Let you sit down there, ma'am, and let that sinner of a cat take his ease on the floor.' Miss Walsh sat down immediately, and I knew what a high opinion she must have had of Mossy Derrane when she allowed him to evict Peter. The cat lashed his tail from the corner where he'd been flung, and spat hatred from his green eyes at the fiddler.

'You might say I'm from the County Galway,' said Mossy. ' Only that I was born on Aranmore in a little place called Gort na gCapall in the west of the island.' I'd thought he had forgotten Brian's question. 'Do any of you know the islands?' he asked then, sweeping us with brilliant fire-filled eyes. None of us did.

'I want to go there some time,' I said. He turned up the wonderful eyes, blazing from a face that might have been cut for a coin, and said:

'You would be happy there, inasmuch as you could be happy anywhere. There's a loneliness in you that God Almighty himself couldn't satisfy, and no man ever will.' He continued to look through my eyes with a wild persistence, and I stared fascinated into his.

---

6   Girl.

'Is it long since you left the islands?' came Brian's voice, as from a great distance, and the fiddler let go my eyes at last and looked into the fire. He moved a sod of turf with his hand and orange light spurted and flooded his face, making the grey hair that curled around the rim of his cap fragile as light.

'It would be thirty years ago,' he said, the evocative beauty of his voice giving you the feel of those years. 'When a man is up against the people of the islands, it is as well for him to go. There is no pardon on the islands for anyone. They thought I was a man better out of the place, and so did I.' The voice was now reflective in rich depths and full of a dim humour.

'What did you do on them, Mossy?' Brian asked, leaning to look into his face but catching only the profile.

'Women,' said the fiddler, splintering into laughter that resounded in the corners of the room. 'Christ, those shy, wild women that could drive a man mad but never disappoint him. I was married at eighteen to a young girl from Killeaney—her name was Barbara Phádraig Bhig, and she had a laugh that would drown all the sorrows of Ireland. A fine wild woman with a blazing head of red hair she was, and a slender body fit for a king. Sometimes there would be dances on the stone flag outside of McDonagh's in Kilronan, and then you'd see her dancing a reel that was like the dancing of stars on a frosty night. Often there would be a crowd of Spanish sailors on shore out of the storm, and then you'd see the devils' black eyes tortured in their heads with watching her and wanting her. One night one of them made for her, and I knocked him over the wall into a high tide to cool his passion for him. They fished him out afterwards, and he screeching like a scalded cat.'

'Did she die on you?' asked Miss Walsh, from the shadow outside the circle of firelight.

'She did not,' the Aran man said; 'but if a man gets the best and tenderest of beef every day of the year for his dinner, do you not think he will grow tired of it, and rather have, maybe, a bit of scrawny bacon for a change? It's the same with women. I knew every twist and turn of Barbara inside of a year, and what good was she to me then? It's the same with all men, but they won't face up to it, only in their own minds. Every Aran man is the keeper of a harem in his mind—did you know that? And that's what drives so many of them to Ballinasloe.'

'Ballinasloe?' murmured Miss Walsh.

'A big asylum that's there,' whispered Brian Clancy.

'The Lord save us!' murmured Miss Walsh again, deeply impressed. Mossy Derrane was smiling now, the corners of his eyes crinkled, elbows on his knees and hands hanging loosely in front of the fire.

'What sort of a girl did you make love to?' prompted Brian.

'No girl at all, but a young woman of thirty that came in the summer to learn Irish. She was a teacher up in Dublin, a lovely black-eyed young woman called Eithne—curse on the second name I can remember— that had a pale face as quiet as a pool sheltered by rocks. She looked like a picture of the Virgin you'd see in a prayer-book, and she had long cool fingers. All the same there was a wildness in her, God bless her. One June day I took her west to Dún Aengus on my father's cart—I would take her everywhere that summer and talk in Irish to her all the time, and she making out she knew every word I was saying. I used to tell Barbara she paid me for it, but I never took any money from her, nor anything else, only what she wanted to give. That day we stayed up on the Dún until all the yellow heat had been drawn out of the sun into the rocks and grass and the grey walls of the fort, and then there was only a weak red sun balanced on the edge of the sky far out over the water to the west, making a bloody track along the sea to the foaming rocks that were three hundred feet below us. We lay on our stomachs on the hot flat ground and dangled our heads over the cliff to watch the white rage of the waves below, splintering over the sharp rocks and sometimes reaching to touch our faces with cold lustful fingers. It was quiet except for the subdued roar of the foam and the call of a gannet or a gull.

'"You're part of this, Muiris," she said, suddenly tilting her white face to mine over the cliff. "I wish I was." I said nothing, only put my mouth to hers and let it lie there, afraid to kiss her. She wasn't afraid. And when we got to our feet, the first nip of night was in the air, and there was a red ribbon along the sky where the sun had been. I looked at her, and it was as if a candle had been lit under her white skin, and her fingers were trembling. "You are like Oisín," she said, in a low voice, and I told her she was Niamh who had come over the seas on a white horse to take him. We lay that night under the inner wall of the fort, and the moon was pale and dim and high when we went riding home in the cart. I was mad with the excitement of her. She stayed for three whole months, and just the same as Diarmuid's and Grainne's beds were all over Ireland, ours were all over Inishmore.'

'Weren't you the divils,' said Miss Walsh, admiringly, 'the pair of you. God help poor Father Tom if he was in the Aran Islands. Tell me, did you never have the priests after you?'

'I did for many a year,' the fiddler said. 'There was only one priest on the big island and he was a terror, only I never took any heed of him so long as the people were with me. But one night in Bungowla I had a fight with Máirtín Sheáin Móir over his wife, a lovely golden woman full of fire, and when I knocked him down on the rocks his head split open.'

'Did he die, the creature?' asked Miss Walsh.

'He did, ma'am, and I knew I would have to take the roads of Ireland after that. The people were up against me, and no man would give me a place in a curragh, and only the young girls would lift their eyes to me passing the road.

'So after Mila Derrane died I got a hooker to Connemara and took the roads.'

'Who was Mila Derrane?' I asked him.

'Mila Derrane was my father, the best fiddler on the big island, and a man that never missed a gathering anywhere. He was never known to sleep with any woman, only my mother, and he was never known to stop talking about women. There was a man had a harem in his mind, surely. The night before he died I watched him, and made Barbara go to her bed. He started to rave about a red princess that he met on the Black Cliffs, and that had promised him to come and marry him in a year and a day. His mind was wandering into all the stories he knew, and no man knew more.

'"Get to sleep and she will come quicker," I said to him, shielding the candle from his eyes.

'"Go to sleep is it and have you get her yourself? I'll not be going asleep until she has kept her promise, the foxy devil." '

'Did you not get the priest for him ? ' asked Miss Walsh, in a hushed voice.

'What good would a priest be to a man like Mila Derrane? Wasn't it a princess he wanted?'

'The Lord save us! ' whispered Miss Walsh. 'Weren't you the terrible man! And he died without oils nor nothing?'

'He died with a laugh on his lips listening to the 'Staicín Orna' that I played for him on his own fiddle—this one before ye on the hearth—and the last thing he said was: "Now you won't get away, you foxy devil."'

'Do you not believe in religion at all, Mossy?' Brian asked him rather unexpectedly.

'I believe, a mhic,[7] in a God of love that has more sense than any of the men in black that try to explain Him to us. I believe that He made me the way I am, for reasons of His own, and that I don't lift a hand that He doesn't know about and permit. I never harmed any man, only Máirtín Sheáin Mhóir, and that was an accident that could happen a bishop.' As he spoke he lifted his fiddle and settled his chin into it.

'What happened Barbara?' asked Miss Walsh, unsatisfied.

'Barbara? Her brother Seán and his wife came to live with her and worked the bit of land. Only for I left he would be in America like the rest of them.'

'Did she mind you going?' Miss Walsh was like a dog with a bone and the fiddler had to drop his bow again with a sigh. He had lost interest in his story; his fingers were itching to play.

'Barbara was a fine woman, ma'am, and didn't she know I had to go? The last thing I saw on Kilronan pier was her standing watching me with the sun on her red hair, and four of the little ones catching at her petticoats.

---

[7]   *My son.*

The older ones wouldn't look at me for many a long day before I left.'

Before he had finished the last sentence he swept the bow along the strings, and the room was full of lament for 'Jimmy Mo Mhíle Stór.' The fiddle had a thin, sweet tone, that seemed to cut mournful patterns in the air, and presently the black cat came soft-footed from the corner and folded himself neatly at the fiddler's side, staring up with green unblinking eyes into the music. I had often heard the lament played before, and a few times since, but I always remember it in that setting— the big Aran man with chin tilted against the fiddle towards the flames, the cat motionless at his feet, the light-filled golden eyes of Brian Clancy fixed on vacancy, the monstrous dark shadow of a listening woman caught in a web of deeper shadows, into which the music dropped slowly, perpetuating the grief of a girl through centuries.

'God bless your hands, Mossy Derrane,' said Miss Walsh very softly, when the fiddler had lifted his head.

''Twas beautiful, Mossy,' Brian said. 'If we could have you on the big night when Bassanio is making his choice, we'd be all right.'

'A play they're doing, Mossy,' explained Miss Walsh, unnecessarily.

'And when will ye be doing it?' the fiddler asked. 'It is a play I always had a great regard for. A man that hath no music in his soul is fit for treasons, stratagems, and spoils—am I right, boy?'

'You are,' Brian smiled. 'We're trying to have it ready for Easter. But sure you might be in Antrim by then?'

'I will not,' the fiddler said, ' but I will be in Aherlow for a while before that, and I could come back to this town again.'

'Will you, then?'

'Surely I will come. I could play this when the young slip says: "Let music sound while Bassanio makes his choice,"' and lifting his fiddle again, Mossy drew from it a delicate little tune that was balanced between gaiety and melancholy, and never made up its mind. It sounded traditional, but I had never heard it before. 'It's beautiful, Mossy. What do you call it?'

'No name at all. It was made by a man called Michael Derrane of Bungowla, the best story-teller on the big island, and a cousin of my own. I heard tell at a fair in Connemara a few weeks ago that the same man is still alive and still telling stories.'

'If I went to Inishmore some summer, Mossy, do you think I could get him to tell me some?'

'I think you could, a chuid.[8] A young girl like you would likely start him without the asking. Let you tell him I played you the tune he made for Cáit Óg's wedding.'

'I will,' I said, and suddenly Brian jumped up and said:

'Even with the talk of the play I forgot the two of us should have been down there, Maeve!'

'It's too late now,' I said, ' and anyhow we can tell them we were getting a musician for the play.'

'True for you,' Brian said, and the fiddler let out a long, rich laugh. 'Anyhow, they'll not lack amusement, never fear.'

'Let the two of you away to your beds now,' Miss Walsh said sleepily, 'and we'll take over that mattress for you, Mossy. What would take you off this time of night?'

'God bless you, ma'am,' the fiddler said, getting to his feet and sending a long, powerful shadow across the ceiling. He took the mattress out of the corner, and spread it beside

---

8   *My dear.*

the hearth, and Peter immediately bounded on to one end and curled himself into a black tight ball. Brian and I said good night, and were going with candles up the narrow steps when he tightened a finger on my arm, and nodded down into the kitchen. Miss Walsh was taking a whisky bottle out of the dresser, and the fiddler was peacefully propped on one elbow before the flames, his long legs stretched the length of the mattress, one toe touching the curled cat.

'A good night to the two of you,' murmured Brian for my ears only, and the candle flame stood in his eyes. 'Bail ó Dhia ar an obair!'[9] Later I was put to sleep by a music that seemed to come out of the heart of the night, and spread itself through the house.

---

9   *God Bless the work!*

VIII

'A panny a bunch the lovely shamrocks, only a panny a bunch.' It was a Dublin voice, low and raucous, coming from somewhere outside the station, and hearing it, I thought: Home. I made my way happily through the crowds of country people up for to-morrow's match in Croke Park, and was glad I had not written to say I was coming. I had always hated being met by the family at stations, the careful waiting smiles, the fuss, the half-answered questions. I stopped outside at the basket of shamrocks and looked at the face above it, a round scrubbed Dublin face, with hair scraped back from it so tightly that you got the impression it might crack. The woman had an apron probably hoarded in its purity for this occasion; in the crook of one arm she held the basket, with the other hand she lifted a bunch of shamrock into my face.

'A panny the lovely shamrocks, only a panny the lot, lady.' I gave her threepence, and she fastened a beautiful fresh sprig into my coat and handed me the rest. Business wasn't so good, because most people were too busy with cases and taxis to bother, so she treated the rare customers well. I thanked her and passed out into the yellow, fading, spring light of the quays. I was wrapped in one of my rare, purely happy moods, when nothing really seemed to penetrate. A man could have throttled another and thrown him over the river wall and I mightn't have noticed. Out of the noisy excitement of Kingsbridge a web of peace and draining light w over the quay. Leaning on the wall, I looked over at the spires of Saint Patrick's and Christchurch passively resisting the darkness. Rooftops and buildings were anonymous, merged in folds of early shadow, but the two spires were still catching long, dim lights from the sky. Over the Liffey gulls wheeled and briefly flashed their gold-stained wings, drifted, touched the water, wheeled again. Farther down the river, Capel Street bridge flung its circular shadow, closing off the light, and farther still, the slender Halfpenny Bridge mirrored itself so perfectly that you fancied it was a black ball poised lightly on the water, and that the slightest wind would send it rolling, air-light, up the river. Dublin was wonderful, like a beautiful woman who never looks the same twice—a hair blown out of place, a scarf twisted to a new angle, and she is different, a mystery perpetuated.

O'Connell Street was gay and incongruous with gaudy neoned twilight veiling the gracious beauty of the white, wide street. Shrill music pierced the chromium doors of ice-cream parlours, luring the happy holiday crowds. Sacrilege, all that chrome and neon vulgarity, against the aloof, flowing loveliness of the GPO, and the white stone faces of the dead who lined the centre of the road. Laughing young men with monstrous growths of shamrock in their coats, and paper hats bearing the colours of their county, linked arms across the width of the paths, and shouted encouragement to teams that tomorrow would take the field in Croke Park.

'Up Munster! '
'Kerry every time! '
'Tiny King will give ye the answer! '
'Up Joe Collins!'

'Up Munster!'

And the next uproarious group, close on the heels of the first, but with hats of a different colour, would shout:

'Up Ulster!'

'Cavan for your life! '

'Up Tommy Reilly! '

'Tiny King will be sorry his mother didn't choke him! '

'Up Ulster every time! '

Cynical Dubliners stood under lampposts and smiled superiorly as each group passed, vastly amused at these bawling, rustic, black-booted invaders of their city. One little man with a hungry white face and a huge cap flung it into the air shouting: ' Up Dubalin! ' There was a heavy roar of laughter from the bystanders. This was the sort of crowd I loved, the sort that always tempts me to linger, just as a brass band always tempts me to follow it. But it was getting late—Clery's clock said ten-to-nine, and I had got off the train at eight o'clock. So I hurried across the road for a bus, but half-way over, a shouting, linked crowd of Kerrymen descended on me, screaming their victory chant, and whizzing around me so fast in a circle that their faces were only confused, red blurs. Finally I ducked under two linked arms, but not before a paper hat had been wedged firmly on my head with the appeal:

'Wear that for luck, a ghrá,[10] and don't let the beads out of your hands tomorrow!'

I missed the bus, and waited ten minutes for another, twirling the hat around on my finger, perfectly happy.

I was glad I had taken the family unawares. Coming up the road that only wakened when a train blundered

---

10   Darling.

by over the bridge, I tried to imagine the scene I would break in on: Bobby on the hearth rug where she always was, father and George Henderson quarrelling in the corner, mother sewing under the lamp, and Sheila with head bent over her books on the table, and Brendan—more than likely Brendan would be out. I wished I could get through a window and break in on their naturalness just like that. But I knocked, and waited, more excited than I had believed one could be coming home. There was a pause and I imagined my mother saying: 'You open the door, Sheila, you're nearest it,' and Sheila lifting a peevish face and protesting 'I opened it the last time and Bobby isn't doing anything important. Let her go.' Next minute I knew I'd been right, because Bobby's racing slippered feet sounded along the hall, and she bumped to a standstill at the door. She always did that. Then the door opened, and Bobby's eyes and mouth were round.

'Maeve!' she breathed, too surprised to shout. I stepped in and closed my fingers over her mouth.

'Don't say a word, Bob, I just want to surprise them.' She nodded her black head and clung to my arm, as if she thought I might run away again. Even in the few months she had lengthened—at least her limbs had, and she was now a leggy little creature in black stockings and a tartan skirt that had got too small for her, with long thin wrists showing far beyond the sleeves of her red jumper. The pale face had got even more remarkably like our mother's, and the most notable thing about it was a pair of long, shining, black eyebrows arching slenderly over the dark eyes. She would be prettier than Sheila, far prettier than I.

'What's keeping Bobby at all?' I heard my mother saying, and Bobby's sharp little cat's teeth flashed in a muffled laugh. Then next minute we were in the room, Bobby still clinging to my arm, and now laughing shrilly.

'Look who's here! ' she shouted, as if that were necessary. There was confusion in a moment.

'Maeve, you sly dog!' That was Brendan, jumping from the armchair he'd been sharing with Máire Lavin.

'Virgin most pure! ' said my mother, not referring to me; that was an expression of hers. 'It's Maeve! '

'Where did you get all the shamrock?' said Sheila, flinging back her plaits when she lifted her head. My father had both my hands in his in a moment, crushing the shamrock.

'You're welcome back, darling,' he said, looking at me intently and rather fiercely—but that was the normal expression of his eyes.

'Where's George?' I asked, ignoring all the other questions; somehow I was disappointed not to see him there. It was as if a familiar chair had been taken away, and the room looked different. My father looked away abruptly, and in the sudden silence, Bobby said:

'He's sick, Maeve, and they wouldn't take me to see him—nobody would,' and she was on the point of bursting into quick tears when my mother said:

'Would you ever run like a pet, Bobby, and put on the kettle for me—Maeve must be starving,' and in the importance of this errand, Bobby's fists came out of her eyes and she ran out down to the kitchen.

'Is George badly ill?' I said, suddenly afraid, vividly seeing the beautiful Custom House before me.

'He's not too well,' Brendan said. 'I'll run you over to see him in the morning.'

'Run me over?' I said, and all together, they began

to tell me about Brendan's Hillman. Máire had pushed me down on to the couch, and was now excitedly talking beside me, a stone angel come alive, with flushed face and tossed shining red hair. Happiness had transformed her—I remembered suddenly the pale, irritatingly modest girl undressing at Portmarnock last summer, and Doreen's laughing remarks.

'But why didn't I hear about this car before?' I said, still looking at Máire.

'I wanted to give you a land when you came home at Easter,' Brendan said. 'You kept this visit up your sleeve.'

'How did you manage a car?' I said.

'Didn't you hear about his promotion?' my mother said.

'Oh, of course. What's this you are, Brendan, Parliamentary Secretary?'

'JEO,' Brendan said, smiling down at Máire.

'I remember,' I said. 'Have you anything else up your sleeve?'

'I'll tell you to-morrow,' he said, and I did not miss Máire's terrified, appealing, upward glance. She had not changed much after all. But later, when she and I were washing up outside (I had protested that I wouldn't feel really at home until I had washed up a few times), she said to me, polishing a shining white plate unnecessarily:

'There's something I want to tell you, Maeve.'

'I'm listening,' I said, unable to resist pulling her leg a bit. She reminded me suddenly of Brendan that night when he had come into my room after the play and shamefacedly asked for an invitation to Kiernan's.

'I want to tell you something,' she began again, biting her lip. She had the red vivid lips common to red-haired people; I had never remembered seeing them rouged.

Laughing, I looked at her, the gold-tipped eyelashes fragile on her cheek, the lip still caught between her teeth. Incredible how a girl my own age, who had grown up in the same environment, should have the cloistral air of a novice, whose eyes saw no farther than the tall candles on the altar.

'I'll get your shamrock from inside and put it out here in water,' she said, turning the innocent luminous eyes into my face and then disappearing. When she came back I was leaning against the dresser, still smiling, and wondering how much longer it was going to take to be told what I already knew. Máire filled a small glass bowl with water and arranged the sprawling small green leaves with slow fingers, which I suddenly noticed were unsteady. She turned around then, bright drops of water still pearling her hands, and for the first time she fixed me seriously with the shining, innocent eyes.

'I don't know how to begin telling you, Maeve,' she said, in a low voice.

'But I know already,' I laughed.

'Know already?' She flushed. 'Did Diarmuid tell you?'

'Diarmuid? Look here, what *are* you talking about, Máire?'

'Since you went away Doreen has been trailing Diarmuid everywhere and everyone knows about it now. They go to dances and theatres and—I told her how mean it was and she only laughed and said that if you cared anything for Diarmuid you wouldn't go away and she was only consoling him. Now her mother is beginning to talk, and she's telling everyone Doreen and Diarmuid are engaged.' Máire brought it all out in a rush, her eyes never leaving my face, her colour deepening with every word. I listened to this confirmation of suspicion as I would listen to the voice of an actress formally making a speech which could not touch me.

'Never mind, Máire. Diarmuid isn't a baby—it will be all right. He can't be rude to Doreen, very well. It doesn't worry me a bit. Do the family know about this?'

'Brendan does, and I'm not sure about your mother.' Máire had uncertainly turned away, as if she had decided to leave something unsaid. Her fingers moved idly again among the shining wet leaves. I tried desperately to remember something I should have said and had forgotten. The thought slipped maddeningly through my brain each time I tried to catch it. Finally I grasped the right thought firmly, closing out every other. Time enough to think later; a lifetime to think.

'Máire, when are Brendan and you becoming engaged?' She didn't turn around; I watched the bright fall of the hair about her shoulders. When she dropped her head slightly at my question, the hair parted at the back and her neck showed white and fragile.

'We're engaged now, only nobody knows. They won't till Easter, and we're getting married in the summer.' Her voice was listless and low, and I remembered, with regret, her radiance when I had broken in on the family. What was it Oona said of the Countess Cathleen?— sorrows that she's but read of in a book prey on her mind as if they were her own. Was that it?

'That's wonderful, Máire. I'm very glad it's you, and so will Mother be too.'

She still did not lift her head, and I said: 'Come and help me finish up that drying and then we'll go in, Máire.' And it didn't seem to me strange that I should be trying to comfort her.

IX

After Mass next morning, when Brendan's Hillman had been emptied of the family and Bobby had mercifully been borne away by a group of Sunday-dressed, green-ribboned little girls down the road, Brendan said to me: 'There's somewhere I want to take you, before we go to Henderson's.'

'Where?'

'You'll see,' he grinned, and the smooth green little car moved away from our house and out on to the main road. Brendan was not very good at corners yet; there had been a bad moment, which I had tactfully ignored.

'Pretty little piece, isn't she, Maeve? And smooth as silk to drive.'

'She's a beauty,' I agreed, watching the stretch of sunny road spinning to meet us. 'How did you get her?'

'Mr. Kiernan was selling her cheaply because Mrs. Kiernan was mad for a bigger car. They've a peach of a new Ford now. Does Nora know you're home?'

'No, I don't think so. She's no good at writing letters —I've only had one since I left, so I didn't bother writing to her.'

'Herself and ma*ma*,' he put the stress laughingly on the last syllable, 'are not getting on too well lately. Nora was over one evening with Máire, and she was full of complaints at being forced to take up a commercial course. She hates it.'

'In the summer she said she didn't mind,' I said. 'Does Doreen ever come to the house?' I tried to sound casual.

'No. College takes up too much of her time, fortunately. Look at the dazzle on that water, Maeve—it would blind you.' I looked across at the spring sunlight splintering the water into glittering choppy fragments, and making the sunny spaces of white cloud look dim by contrast. People strolled about the grass fringing the rocks, and children ran screaming after dogs, or chased each other. Brendan and I used to play here in Clontarf as children ourselves. I wished he would not be such a fool, sparing my feelings. That was what I hated.

'A good driver can't afford to admire the effects of sun on water or anything else,' I said unpleasantly, and he turned the monkish face to me with a grin, the sun striking brilliantly on the dark-rimmed spectacles.

'I'm not a good driver, Maeve. Did I ever tell you about the three drunks who came in one night into the Boot Inn?'

'Yes.'

'Well,' his eyes were on the road again, his hands lying relaxed on the wheel, 'one of them gets as far as the counter and then flops on to it with outstretched arms. The second fellow collapses on to a stool, and the third only just gets past the door, and then drops on the ground singing.'

'Two large whiskies,' says the fellow at the counter, lifting his head to the barman.

'Two?' says the barman. 'And what about your friend over at the door?'

'Never mind him,' says the fellow, 'he's had enough. He has to drive us home.'

As often before, I laughed at Brendan's solemn recital of the chestnut, his voice even and monosyllabic, one piece of dialogue run into the next.

'Good, isn't it?'

'Marvellous. Where are we going, Brendan?' I glanced out at the long sunny arm of the Bull Wall reaching out into the bay, at the little flying villas running into the distance on the other side, out of sight.

'You'll see,' said Brendan again, pressing the accelerator suddenly and sending the little car speeding straight into the sun, it seemed.

Rapid movement I have always loved, and by the time we got out of the car, almost under the velvet shadow of Howth, I could have shouted or sung to work off the excess of sudden blazing delight.

'It's spring,' I said obviously, touching with a finger the long curled buds of a chestnut tree, which dropped a slender branch over our heads across the footpath.

'Yes,' Brendan said, taking my hand, and pulling me past the tree and through the scattered bricks until we stood before a half-built house, roofless, naked-looking in the sun.

'Ours,' he said. 'Máire's and mine.'

There were three houses being built together, houses that would have long slanting roofs and curving bay windows. You could see the shape of the window frames all right, and through them you could see the white fresh rafters stretching up slantwise to the roof, like human bones, I thought. The place was an ugly desolation at the moment, cement bags everywhere, and fine white dust and scattered bricks and churned red earth. But Brendan, you could see, was looking at the finished house, seeing fresh curtains lifted by a breeze, smelling carnations and stock and freshly mown grass on long summer evenings, seeing Máire laughing in a white dress. He suddenly remembered me, and his dark-spectacled eyes stopped wandering over the chaos as over an enchanted country, and smiled uncertainly at me. I remembered seeing him look like that once years ago, when as a pale, studious-looking little boy he had built a crane from a Meccano set and was showing it to Mother for the first time.

'It will be beautiful, Brendan,' I said. 'You're lucky. Are you buying it?'

'Oh, yes,' he said, as if the question were of no importance. 'Through the Civil Service Building Fund. Two thousand five hundred. Come in till you see the drawing-room,' and he led me through the gap that would be a door, through a wide space, and through another gap. The place smelled of mortar, despite the free access of air. But it would be a good-sized room, even beautiful, because of the wide, curving, bay window.

'We're having bookshelves along this wall,' Brendan was saying, pointing to a naked strip of wall, the plaster of which was not even dry,' and heavy green curtains up there. Máire wants nearly everything green. I like it too.'

'It's because of her hair,' I said, half listening to him and looking up through the white rafters into the sky, across which one woolly cloud floated. This house would grow with the leaves, spring day by spring day, and when those narrow, quickening buds exploded soundlessly in the sun, it would be nearly finished, and when white candles lit the wide green leaves in summer, it would be a home, with Máire moving through the rooms, her cloistral air gone, perhaps, lost on a night in summer. Or would passion change her? Probably not. She was one of those people whose lives are candles shielded from every wind, who move effortlessly to their predestined end, untouched by anything. Other people fumbled their way to peace; she was quietly propelled towards it, almost without volition. I had known, although she hadn't, when I watched Brendan and her going up the wide staircase in Kiernan's that night, singularly apart from the coloured crowd, that they would marry. I knew now that they would be happy, because of the shielding fingers around the candle. I knew there would be children in this house, dark little serious girls like Brendan, shouting red-haired boys with eyes like Máire's.

'Maeve, there's something I think you should know,' Brendan said, turning his eyes to me and blinking.

'For God's sake, Brendan, don't stand there blinking like the sort of fool who tells kids that babies come from gooseberry bushes. I know what you're going to tell me, and I'm sick of being told. I know Doreen is going around with Diarmuid, and I don't give a damn. I've known for weeks. For God's sake put all ideas of breaking it gently to me out of your head.'

'I'm sorry, Maeve,' he said, amazingly calm and gentle. I remembered his rages as a child, the hairbrush he had once thrown at me for saying he was afraid to go downstairs in the dark. 'Forgive me for interfering. But I don't think you know everything. Doreen,' he said, moving over to the window, 'is going to have a child.'

'I know.' I lied, driving my nails into the palms of my hands. Don't let him be sympathetic or I shall tear him.

'I didn't think you did,' he said tiredly. 'Nobody would yet, only her mother is doing so much blowing. She's insisting on a marriage.'

'Why not?' I said. 'She's entitled to that surely?' If I could get out somewhere on a height, with a cold wind blowing in my face—Howth, yes, why not Howth? You couldn't keep away from places for ever.

'Let's get back,' Brendan said, drained suddenly of joy, as Máire had been last night. So that was what she had withheld? Prudish little mouse. Couldn't bring herself to tell me. Little idiot.

'Not home,' I said, carelessly. 'You said we'd go to see George. I'd like to.'

'All right,' Brendan said, tiredly still, walking slowly out with me through the scattered builders' rubble into the sunlight. I remember the look of the signboard in front of the house—white large lettering on a black board: Thomas Larkin, Building Contractor, Oaklands, Cloncliffe Road, Dublin. I know that road. Which house is it? It doesn't matter.

I remember little of the drive back except the thick excited crowds everywhere on the roads, all making their way to the match, to sit for hours with sandwiches and excitement as their only nourishment. I remember, too, the fact that I talked all the time; of what, I have not the slightest recollection. I remember how carefully Brendan drove, because of the crowds, and how once a paper hat with Munster colours sprang up against the bonnet of the car, and the brakes ground us to a standstill. I gripped the narrow ledge of the window and broke a finger-nail with the jolt.

The knocker of George's house was muffled with a strip of brown silk and thudded softly when we knocked. The door was opened by one of George's pale, tall sisters—I never knew which was which. They both had cold, colourless faces and severe hair styles, and an air of frigid virginity. Their names were cold—Edith and Maud. She led us almost silently up the long flight of stairs and paused a moment before George's door. Then she tapped on a panel with dry, white fingers, and opened the door, hesitating slightly as if wondering if she should let us in by ourselves. Finally, she stood and motioned us in, and afterwards we heard the door closing softly behind us and her softer feet going downstairs. Brendan walked over to the bed where everything, even the eiderdown, was white, and I stood uncertainly at the door, suddenly released from the web of my own thoughts and terrified by the immobile, worn, white face on the pillow. I was vaguely aware of an oppressive heat in the room, of daffodils splashing the dimness of one corner, of a small fire struggling with sunlight that struck through dark, half-drawn curtains.

'How is the form, George?' Brendan was asking, lifting the bloodless hands off the eiderdown. How could he ask such a futile, shallow question in a voice so impudently casual? He is dying, I thought, terrified. I had never come close to death before, never before seen a living face hollowed and altered into the image of death.

'Maeve is up for the day, George,' Brendan was explaining, looking impatiently over his shoulder at me lingering still at the door. I forced myself across the room, and shivered at the touch of the big wasted hand, and when I tried to smile down into the strange face on the pillow my own face seemed to have stiffened, to be out of control.

'How are you, George?' My voice sounded like somebody else's—like the voice of somebody speaking out loud in church. George, I kept thinking, horrified— George, you used to dance at tennis club dances on summer nights and flirt with the prettiest girls. You went to war for the fun of it—I know, because of the way you look in that photograph on the piano. You used to be full of life even when you were wounded— you've shouted at my father over politics as long as I can remember. You belong to that corner at home—it wasn't like home last night. George!'

'Patsy?' George spoke my father's name with difficulty, opening the dry, white lips several times before any sound came. The big gaunt face was eager for a moment. I realised how little any of us meant to him, except my father, and it saddened me.

'He's coming this evening, George, and he'll stay as long as you want him,' Brendan said.

Afterwards, going home, I couldn't shake off the vague dread that caught me in the shaded warm room full of death. A part of my secure youth would slip away with that life, and then the first defence would have broken down. There was a note from Diarmuid waiting when I got home, asking me to meet him in town at three. I twirled the paper idly in my fingers, suddenly drowned in a sense of loss, of which Diarmuid was only a part.

X

A day might only have elapsed since our last meeting, instead of nearly three months. He was smiling (the remembered smile like a match-flame playing from eyes to mouth, from mouth to eyes) and he took one of my hands in both of his, feeling it as one feels for something in a dark room. It wasn't true. Nothing can have happened. He would look different. He said: 'Maeve,' almost without expression, not like a greeting. I said nothing, only ran my eyes from the yellow hair to the brown shoes, beside my brown shoes. Then my eyes travelled up again to the narrow fingers enclosing my hand. They were softer than a woman's, softer than mine.

'Where shall we go, Maeve? Howth?'

'No, not Howth. Enniskerry.'

The undertone did not escape him, and it registered in the lines of his mouth for an instant. Then he smiled slowly down at me and nodded. We went across the bridge for a bus, in shrouded sunlight, and looking down the river I saw widening shadows of clouds gradually closing in on sunny spaces. To avoid linking him I put both hands in my pockets, but before we had passed Hawkins Street his left hand was in my pocket, lightly closing over mine. If I liked, I thought, I could free my hand and crush his like a leaf. Contact was dangerous; the carefully built-up hatred I had strengthened all the way into town in the bus was crumbling. I relaxed every muscle in my hand to suggest indifference. He might have been holding an empty glove.

'I thought you'd be at the match today,' I said idly.

'I did think of going,' he answered, 'but then I didn't know you'd be up.'

'No. Who told you?'

'One of your sisters.' Everybody is kind. Couldn't they all mind their own business and leave me alone? Better never to have felt that hand again. Nobody, ever again, would put as much into a hand-touch as Diarmuid, a delicate muted excitement, the transmission of a thought too frail to be conveyed in speech. We stepped on a bus, and, running upstairs, I felt the palm of my hand with the fingers curiously, half expecting it to feel different. We sat in the back seat.

'How is college?' I said. I felt a stubborn desire to ward off any explanation, any discussion, and as I watched the thoughts passing across the delicate face beside me, I was determined not to let them escape. He paused, seeming to pass judgment on the futility of the question, and then the conductor came—'Please.' Diarmuid took a handful of coins from his pocket, cupping them in one hand, selecting a half-crown with the curving narrow fingers of the other; the old gesture, commonplace, trivial, infused for me only with the formal grace of a movement in a ballet. Absurd to give way now to the flooding nostalgia. Yet why had I come? Because the thought of refusing had never occurred to me, I answered myself.

'Kew,' said the conductor, passing on, and Diarmuid replaced the money in his pocket and said:

'College?' He thought a moment, folding the two white tickets together in half, then quartering them, and stroking them gently between first and second fingers.

Then he glanced quickly into my face, looked away, and began to talk of a literary society, of which he was apparently chairman. He had written a paper on Joyce for it, which had gone down badly because he had refused to admit that any passage in *Ulysses* could be described as pornographic. He said that fragment we had wondered about (did I remember?) was in *Ulysses* after all, and that it described smoke coming from chimneys in Kildare Street. He gave an amusing description of the secretary's speech on the conclusion of his paper. This girl was evidently a pillar of the Legion of Mary. All the time as he spoke, I got the impression that he was speaking something carefully rehearsed, rehearsed for an emergency. And all the time he stroked the rolled tickets, sometimes opening them out and then rolling them again.

When we got out of the bus in the little hollowed village of Enniskerry, pretty as a postcard Alpine hamlet, the sun was shining strongly, and the clouds were high and white and racing before a warm wind that smelled of buds and turned earth.

We struck up the steep hill opposite the Powerscourt Arms, under the tossed expectant trees. Who was it who had said that a spring wind was full of cold lust? It wasn't true. It was full of a passionless joy. We had only come up this road once before, two years ago, with copies of Macbeth under our arms because we both had speeches to learn for the following day. Diarmuid had had to learn: 'My way of life is fallen into the sere ... ' and I, the passage beginning: 'Come, sealing night, scarf up the tender eye of pitiful day ... ' We had walked, ankle-deep, through the estate woods, and sat on a fallen tree to learn the lines.

'Do you remember the chubby little boy scout with the pale face that kept staring at us?' said Diarmuid, and I knew that once again we'd been thinking together.

'Yes, and you said: "Thou cream-faced loon, where gottest thou that goose-look?" like Macbeth to whatever-his-name-was.'

'God, yes,' Diarmuid said, laughing for the first time, with a quick jerk of the head and a glitter of teeth. 'And he ran away through the trees shouting: "Yez are both mad."'

'Let's go through the estate again,' I said, with an eagerness I couldn't have explained.

'Why?' The dark, mature eyes were glancing down unclouded into my face, as if a film had been dissolved because he had won. The superficial crust of conversation had been broken.

'I don't know. That day, maybe,' I said, smiling when I remembered the row there had been at home. ('No daughter of mine will go traipsing around the woods at nine o'clock at night. Oh, no, begod. With a little bowsey that should get his bottom reddened for him by his father.') I could still hear my father's voice, and hear mother's: 'Now listen, Patsy,' just like poor George would say. 'I got into a blazing row at home that night,' I said.

'Me, too,' Diarmuid smiled. We went through the high gates, with the symbolic eagle poised above them, and Diarmuid gave two sixpences to the ex-soldier porter in exchange for two white tickets.

'The Big House,' Diarmuid murmured, glancing at the tickets. 'Sic transit.' And then his mind played back again two years, as mine was doing. 'That day seems an age ago. Were we really only seventeen? And are we really only nineteen?'

We were, but already change had touched us; change and the passing of things we had considered inviolable. We walked on silently into the woods.

'Forgive me, Maeve,' he said suddenly, 'if you can.' He stood still under a lime tree, not looking at me, tracing the bark with vague fingers. Watching him, slender and tall and young, under a young bare tree, I thought suddenly that in him was all mortal beauty, fumbling and fragile and doomed. For the moment I did not consider what he was asking me to forgive, or if forgiveness were possible. I was looking at him from too great a distance.

'God, what a mess!' he said, a shadow of distaste and weariness passing over his face. The commonplace phrase recalled me with a jerk to reality. How many people all over the world were saying that, and for the same reason? A hatred caught me, for Diarmuid and his weakness, for Doreen and her slyly dressed, provocative body that had traded on the weakness.

'You might perhaps tell me how it all happened?' I tried to keep the hatred out of my voice. I didn't succeed, evidently, because he winced, and the straight mouth dropped almost imperceptibly at the corners. But I didn't care. I was full of Stephen Dedalus's cold, lucid indifference. And I wanted to hurt him, to watch every word reflecting on his face. I dropped down on the dry, turfy ground under the tree, and fastened my arms around my knees, never taking my eyes off his face.

'Even before you went away, Maeve, she had a habit of following me around. We attend the same lectures, and she had plenty of opportunities. She always managed to sit beside me, even breaking in and excusing herself to Sean and Donal and the lads. She never sat with girls. I didn't mind much at first, because I knew she was a friend of yours. And anyhow, she was amusing, and witty in a way, and very easy on the eyes. And I didn't see how I could prevent her, if she wanted to sit beside me. I'm sorry if all this sounds unnecessarily condemning. What followed finally was my fault entirely, and don't think I'm making any attempt to prove otherwise. But what I am trying to do is to tell you as accurately as I can what led up to it. Do you understand?'

'Yes, I understand.'

'Well, some time in November she told me her father had got two tickets for a dance in the Gresham, and asked me to go with her. A dress affair. I was honestly surprised, and of course refused, saying that I'd be going somewhere with you. She wasn't at all put out. Said she thought I'd have liked to come.

'You never mentioned it to me,' I said.

'I didn't see that it would do any good, Maeve. And I had no occasion to mention it since I'd refused. But the incident made me uneasy. That was why I was so concerned when you told me you were going away. While you were there, nothing could have happened. I saw you every day, and I never wanted anyone else, nor do I now. Even the thought of intimacy with another girl never occurred to me. But then when you were gone, it was different. I was horribly alone, and uneasy. I couldn't mistake the meaning in Doreen's eyes, and I knew myself for what I was. At night sometimes I used to beg you out loud to come back—with some confused memory of Rochester and his voice reaching to Jane Eyre.'

'But why didn't you write and ask me?'

'Pride. You'd chosen freely to go away. As a matter of fact, when I watched that train carrying you out of the station, and ran after it to see you as long as I could, I fully intended to ask you. That night when I went home I did, but I tore up the letter the next morning. I imagined your laughing, calling me a clinging fool. I'm sorry I wasn't.' He paused, as if he expected me to say something, but I was silent. He reached for a blade of grass and stroked it slowly, as he had stroked the tickets. We listened to the wind moving with thin sounds through the budded trees.

'Then the day after you went I was walking through the Green with Donal Carson. My gloves were sticking out of one pocket—you know I hardly ever wear them. In a second somebody had snatched them, and when I turned round I saw Doreen racing away through the trees past the bridge, looking back over one shoulder and laughing. It was such a silly trick, childish and ridiculous. But I ran after her. When I caught her up I tried to wrest the gloves from her without hurting her hands. She snatched them behind her back, and said: "Kiss me and you'll get them back. But you wouldn't dare." It was so absurd that I drew back, laughing at her. Her eyes snapped, and she dropped the gloves on the ground, and suddenly fastened her arms around me and kissed me. Not childish kisses. "Now you can have your rotten gloves," she said. "Good-bye, Diarmuid, you're the goods." Then she ran off.' He paused again, and I remembered Doreen at parties, years ago, cheating at Postman's Knock and Spin-the-Bottle, to get the boy she wanted.

'The day after that, she called at the house and asked me to go to a party out in Terenure, given by friends of her family. I know now that I was mad to go. But I was fed up and had nothing to do, and her kissing me had touched me—in a way. But, anyhow, I went. It was one of those ghastly affairs with cocktails and dancing and tinsel girls, and a hired band. I regretted going before we'd been there an hour. After a dance, Doreen whispered, "I'm terribly bored. Come on outside," and she led the way into the cool hall and then she opened another door farther down, and switched on the light. She knew her way around the house well. It was a chilly little living room. She went over and switched on the electric fire, one of those things with mock-coals. She stood laughing at me with her back to the fire. She had on a silver dress, with a slit that showed all of one leg, and another slit at the throat— or rather it began at the throat.'

'I know it,' I said, half to myself.

'Well, she said she was hot and took out a diamond clasp that held the edges together. Then she asked me to sit down, and asked me was I afraid of her. That's how it happened. It was partly because I wanted to teach her a lesson, to frighten her—I learned that she couldn't be frightened—and partly because she was lovely, and she'd maddened me standing there laughing.'

'Was that the only time?' I spoke quietly because anger and jealousy were gripping me, and searing contempt for Diarmuid. The fool. Doreen had thrown herself at him, for amusement, for devilment, and he had caught her. She'd been doing that since she was fourteen, not giving herself to people then, but doing everything except that. And that night at Kiernan's party, she'd come down the stairs with the Moore boy and looked at us with a faint, smiling superiority, from a higher plane of experience. That was the first time.

'There were a few other similar occurrences under similar circumstances,' Diarmuid said. 'There's no point in going into more details. It didn't take me long to get sick with myself, and curse myself for writing to you just the same every day. So I stopped the letters and tried to shake off Doreen, but it wasn't easy. Now it's harder.'

'Why?'

I knew the reason, I wanted to hear it again from him. 'She's going to have a child,' he said, tossing the blade of grass away. 'At least she says she is and I suppose it's true. It must have been almost instantaneous, which is unusual.' His cold, hopeless voice infuriated me. I hated him.

'You needn't think you're the only person she obliged,' I said.

'I know that,' he said tiredly. If only he would be angry. If only I could hurt him so much that he would have to show it. 'She told me about him, when I asked. But it couldn't be that,' he ended.

'So you're going to marry her?'

'No,' he said, surprised. 'I'm going to marry you.'

'Me? That's good, Diarmuid. That's really funny. It's funnier than anything in *Dublin Opinion*.' When I laughed he caught me roughly by the arms and I felt the thin sharp fingers pressing to the bone. His angry dark eyes were so close that I blinked, and the delicately cut face was transformed with rage. I was glad, glad. I laughed into his face and he shook me until my hair came loose and was drawn back by the wind. He let go suddenly and cupped my face in his fingers. The colour was gone from his cheeks and his mouth was defenceless.

'I love you, Maeve, do you hear? I love you.' I sprang free and got to my feet.

'You have a most original way of showing it.'

'I asked you not to go away,' he said, like a child repeating a lesson. 'I begged you.'

'And because I did, you thought you'd teach me

a lesson, I suppose?' He didn't reply and my remark seemed to me cheap and stupid. The yellow hair was so close I could have touched it, ruffling it as I had often done, and then combing it with my fingers. Never, never again. He stood up.

'You can't ask me to believe it's all over, Maeve?'

'I'm not asking you to believe anything. I'm simply telling you I won't marry you. You've committed yourself through your own fault, as you said. You're responsible for that child, and for Doreen. Take them.'

'I don't love her. She doesn't love me.'

'It's a bit late to discover that now.'

'There's no question of discovering it now. Surely it was obvious from what I told you that love never entered the business. You're not stupid.'

'It's good to know that.' Angrily he reached for a perfect curled bud above our heads and tore it from the branch.

'You're merciless,' he said bitterly. 'You look at me all the time from the heights of your virginity, and smile and despise and condemn me. I can see it in your eyes.'

'You hardly expected me to applaud the deed. But I certainly don't condemn you—why should I? It's your own business. All I'm doing is advising you to marry Doreen because she's entitled to it. She has a claim now that completely shadows mine, if I ever had one, or if anyone can be said to have a claim on anyone else, short of Doreen's.' He didn't answer, but tore the bud to pieces with vicious deliberation. He threw the pieces down and ground them with his heel. His violence was out of proportion to the frail thing he was destroying.

'For the last time, will you marry me?'

'No.'

'I know you.' He was white with bitterness. 'You're merciless and proud and stubborn, and your pride has been damaged. That's why you won't marry me. You're trying to make yourself believe it's out of concern for Doreen, but it's not. And the tragedy is you'll regret it.'

'I'm learning. I never noticed before that you were conceited.'

'It isn't conceit, and you know it. It's just that I'm sure about every part of you, more sure than you are yourself. And I know we belong together in mind and body for ever. We belonged before we were born.'

'I have to catch a train at seven.'

His eyes closed a moment, and when he looked up again his face was almost indifferent. 'We'll go now, Maeve.'

We walked back through the trees silently. My hands were in my pockets, his stiffly at his sides. When we got back to town, the Munster men were filling the streets with their yells of victory.

Part Three

THE THIRD DEATH

Many times man lives and dies
Between his two eternities,
That of race and that of soul,
And ancient Ireland knew it all.
Whether man die in his bed
Or the rifle knocks him dead,
A brief parting from those dear
Is the worst man has to fear.
Though grave-diggers' toil is long,
Sharp their blades, their muscles strong,
They but thrust their buried men
Back in the human mind again.

W. B. YEATS

I

One evening in April I was down by the river with a thick copybook under my arm. It was a diary which, after five years, was still not finished. That was because I never wrote in it except when I was uncontrollably happy, or equally miserable. I dropped down on the damp grass and flicked through the pages, feeling vaguely that I was touching parts of my life that were gone for ever. The curled pages opened at a passage written in pale, watery, school ink, and I remembered staying in the empty classroom one summer's day at lunchtime to write it. I remembered the laughter, softened by distance into a vague melancholy, coming up to the window from the playground. One was very alone and bitter at thirteen. Still, why exactly had I written this? The reason was lost. I re-read it indifferently:

'I hate women. I hate them so much that when a woman touches me, even for a second, I want to wash and then go out into a clean wind for a walk. Absurd that I should be a woman myself. If I'd only been born a man, even a stupid, ugly man, I think I would wish for nothing else. If Sister C. ever again bends down to me, as she did to-day, so that I can feel her breath on my face, and if she ever closes her fingers around my arm, as she did to-day, I think I'll never come to school again. Never.'

I turned on the limp pages, aware of the warmth touching my cheeks when a wind blew across the river, and of the small sounds of nesting birds. It seemed as if the looped bridge closed off every sound of the town below. I turned on, not reading anything else, until I came to a blank space. I propped the book on my knees and wrote:

   'I think if it were autumn I shouldn't be so full of despair. It's the indifferent cruelty of young leaves, and warm, fertile air, that I can't tolerate. They are so many impertinent intrusions on sorrow. Last night before getting into bed, I stayed for a long time looking at a white-faced moon through cloudy glass, and I shut my eyes and leant my face against the cold smooth surface, and felt the glass with the palms of my hands, and thought: "If you were here ... " This is strange, because he hasn't been close like this for a long time, not since Saint Patrick's Day. She has, though. I've thought of the bubble doubling and redoubling itself insidiously in the darkness of her body, taking on with every day a grotesque semblance of life. I don't regard it as a potential child, but rather as canker growing between me and everything worthwhile. The thought that she will suffer is evilly attractive to me at the moment. This is neurosis. Ludicrous self-indulgence, like kicking a bedpost that has hurt one's toe. It wasn't her fault. It was his. Remember the guilty, weak, hopeless face under the branches of the tree. All right, hate him. But better still, forget all about it. While memory holds a place in this distracted globe—who had said that? Macbeth? No, Hamlet. It was, wasn't it?'

   What is happiness? An attitude of mind imposed on circumstances. All right. Impose it. Somewhere, everyone had a shining, inviolable place in his mind that nothing could touch. When that intruded itself on exterior misery you got happiness, or indifference. Or were they the same? Was all happiness a kind of imperviousness? And now could you talk sense?

I had stopped writing long ago, impatient of the words on paper. Writing things like that got you nowhere, solved nothing. I laid down the book on the wet grass and trailed my fingers through the water. It was warm, because all day long the sun had lain there. I splashed my face, and when the next wind came across the river I was cold. I took up the diary and walked back along the banks into the town. I would be late for rehearsal. If Brian Clancy asked me why, I could say I had been writing. And if he asked me what? I suddenly felt like laughing.

They were all in the schoolhouse when I got there. It was the Casket Scene, and Brian was at the bottom of the classroom with one foot on the seat of a desk, balancing a book on his knee, and shouting at Peter McManus, who was choosing a casket with his back to where the audience would be.

'Will you turn round out of that and let the people see a bit more of you than your backside?' he was saying, and I wondered if he expected Bassanio to choose without looking at the caskets. It appeared he did. Brian's style of production was somewhat outdated; no Reverend Mother in any girls' school could have insisted more determinedly on the players keeping their faces rigidly towards the audience.

'Why are you late, Maeve?' he interrupted himself. 'I thought you were only going to post a letter?'

'So I was, and so I did. But I went for a walk afterwards. Do you want details of it? '

'All I want at the moment is for you to get up on that stage and put that fellow out of pain. Step down you now, Bridie, and be ready for your own entry. Now are you right?'

Nobody ever thought of questioning him. Even Michael Tilson, once the danger of producing *The Playboy* had been removed, was willing to accept the schoolmaster's authority. Apart from an incomprehensible desire to have the actors facing the audience all the time, Brian was not a bad coach. He had done wonders with the slow, thick, southern accent; he had even twisted it to a resemblance of his own rhythmical Kerry tones. Better than this, he had infected everyone with his own vivid enthusiasm. Bridie McMahon, who was wont to spend most nights with her head tilted against Peter McManus's in the local cinema, never missed a rehearsal. Peter never did either, because cinema-going on his own did not attract him. Peter had been given the part of Bassanio—deservedly, because he was a dark, stickily handsome youth who reeked of brilliantine, and had a pair of ardent foolish dark eyes very suitable to the part. Peter's voice was the best thing about him. It was soft and clear, coloured slightly by his birthplace, Tyrone. I liked it.

'I think we could start that over again,' Brian was saying, 'now that you've come. Off the stage, everyone.' Bridie McMahon, who had been taking my part so that the scene could go on, nudged me, and laughed with the merry eyes.

'Let you take him on now,' she said, 'and see can you make a job of him.'

Bassanio, across at the other side of the stage, was surreptitiously combing back his oily, waving hair, and paused to languish a look over at Bridie. The bell sounded then and we walked on to the stage. Brian always kept a small press-bell at his side, and sounded that when he wanted a change in any rendering. It was always sounding.

> *I pray you tarry, pause a day or two*
> *Before you hazard, for in choosing wrong*
> *I lose your company.*
> *There's something tells me, but it is not love …*

It was strange how easily the cream walls of the classroom widened, and the languishing bank clerk, with hand resting on the back of the teacher's chair, became the playboy Bassanio, and Michael Tilson a red-headed Gratiano, and Maureen Walsh a Nerissa denied every beauty but beauty of voice. Her voice was beautiful, full of melody and humour, and full, too, of a youth her face would never have, although she was fifteen. The bell sounded angrily.

'Declare to God Almighty you were never as hopeless as to-night. Look, Maeve, you're supposed to be playing with that fellow, flirting as gloriously as no woman in Shakespeare ever flirted before, and you might be telling him about your grandmother's asthma, for all the flirtation there's in your voice. Listen, woman:

> *There's something tells me, but it is not love,*
> *And you know yourself hate counsels not*
> *In such a quality, I would not lose you.*

'The voice drops for "and you know yourself," etc. Have you got that? All right, begin again. And Peter, you could drum your fingers on the back of her chair —you're nervous as hell, remember. God keep Father Tom away from here to-night,' he ended, half to himself. Immediately there was uproar. Shylock shot out from the wings, pale as death.

'Mister Clancy, the priest isn't coming here to-night? And we not ready nor nothing, Mister Clancy?'

'Janey!' Jessica was saying, hopping up and down in the middle of the stage, where she had no right to be. Bridie McMahon was Jessica. She did a vague little dance with excitement, the sequins on her dress suddenly coming alive with the movements. Everyone was talking to everyone else, until a few furious jabs of the bell brought silence.

'Get back to hell to your places!' Brian shouted, exactly as he would to his class, and the frightened silence continued. 'How the blazes do you expect to act before the whole town at Easter if you're afraid of acting before Father Tom now? Will you answer me that?'

'I'd rather act before the Pope himself,' Michael Tilson said feelingly, 'than before Father Tom.'

'True for you,' came all the voices, and Brian said:

'If you're not all careful the Abbey Theatre will be snapping you up under contract. A lovely pack of sheep, the lot of you! Yerra, get back there, and begin the scene all over again, you God-forsaken pack!'

We began again, and proved rather worse than the last time. Peter's soft northern voice was, I imagine, inaudible to all but me, and I stumbled a few times because of the hushed horrified tones of the ladies-in-waiting behind me.

'I'll die if he comes in.'

'True as God I'll throw a fit.'

The bell sounded again, this time seriously angry. 'Begin that from the entry. Bassanio, it would be an idea to let the people hear what you're saying. And stand more to the left, so that we'll see your face when you're talking to Portia. Yes, that's right. You must be drunk to-night, the whole lot of you. When I ring the bell—'

When he got as far as that, the door opened, and Father Tom stepped in, spinning his stick in one hand, and nodding his head agreeably in all directions, like a visiting celebrity, which indeed he was. The intense blue eyes took in everything. He was so sparely and flexibly built that one imagined him more easily on the playing field.

'And how are we getting on to-night?' Everyone stood as if frozen to the stage. Michael Tilson ran two hands despairingly down his sides, looking as if he wished the red doublet would miraculously give place to his navy serge. Bridie put a round-eyed face around the corner of the stage, her mouth shaped for a 'Janey!'

Brian only seemed utterly unperturbed. He inserted a slip of paper casually and unhurriedly in his book and came up through the desks to the priest. He was the happiest-looking person in the room. Laying an arm lightly on the priest's shoulder, he said something, and Father Tom nodded quickly and affably. The next moment he was laughing and the schoolmaster was joining in. Bridie withdrew her face and Peter McManus whispered to me: 'Mr. Clancy could have the English and the Germans sobbing on each other's necks, so he could after that, if he liked. Do ye mind the wee merry face of His Reverence?'

The next minute the schoolmaster was down at the end of the room, touching the bell, and Father Tom sat down on the top of one of the desks—a thing he detested people doing. 'We'll have that scene again from the beginning,' Brian said. 'Straight through without a stop. Ready.'

Everybody was, of course, incredibly bad. Poor Peter's hand trembled violently at the back of my chair. Bridie told me afterwards that he and she had been chased home by Father Tom the previous night. Bassanio would have had no chance had Father Tom been P.P. of Belmont. But the misfortunes came to a climax when Salerio stretched out his hand to deliver the letter from Antonio, only to discover that he had omitted to provide himself with a letter. A frenzied dumbshow ensued, and Bassanio galloped his lines. So did I mine, being caught up in the general terror. I got a glimpse of Brian Clancy's eyebrows drawing ominously together, and I slowed up.

'Diction very creditable, Mister Clancy,' said Father Tom, when we had limped to the end. 'Very creditable indeed.' His loud patronizing voice was in ludicrous contrast to his thin face, clever-looking and intense. 'But that was only to be expected,' he went on. 'This Society, with the proper disposition, will be a credit to the town yet. A credit, and a valuable source of income for the missions. With the proper disposition, I say. But no group of young people can hope to form themselves into a good energetic healthy team of actors and actresses if they keep the bad hours some of you, I regret to say, seem to favour. I appeal to the Sodality Prefects, to you Michael Tilson, and to you Martha Dowd, to assert your authority in the interests of the Society, and of the town. No group of clean-living young men and women should be seen talking and tricking in the streets after ten o'clock at night. Bid good night to your companions here in the schoolhouse, and then hurry back to your homes without delay, girls with girls, and boys with boys. No decent Catholic boy has any respect for a girl who is willing to dawdle around the streets with him till twelve o'clock at night, and no decent Catholic girl has any business with a boy who expects that of her. It's not in the streets that Christian marriages are made, remember that. Mister Clancy will agree with me, I know that.'

Mr. Clancy's eyes agreed vaguely above the folds of a white handkerchief hastily applied to his nose. Satisfied, Father Tom turned again to the stage and reminded the actors that the Men's Sodality would meet next Sunday, and then took his leave. I marvelled at the intuition behind Brian's choice of play.

He was deeply depressed on the way home. 'What's the use of ever trying to make anything of them, Maeve, when you have a holy father (that they're all in mortal dread of) bursting in every now and then and stifling any bit of life they have?'

'I'm not under the influence of Father Tom and I didn't please you so much either.'

'You'll mend,' he said, with a quick smile. "Tisn't repression that's the matter with you. It's something else.'

'What?'

'It will keep,' he smiled again.

'Anyhow,' I said, 'you seem to have the mistaken idea that it's necessary to have experienced a sensation before expressing it on the stage.'

'And you seem to have the mistaken idea that it's not.'

'Take Jane Austen,' I said, ' who knew as much about the vagaries of passion as de Maupassant and yet didn't have to lead his sort of life to come by the knowledge.'

'Writers are different,' he said. 'They're born. Actors are built. If you take the case of—'

At this point running feet sounded behind us, and turning around, we found Maureen Walsh behind us, breathless, flushed, holding Brian's scarf up to him.

'You left this. I mean, you left this behind you. I thought I'd—' She stopped and gazed beseechingly up at him, rouged lips slightly open. She blinked several times.

'Thanks very much, Maureen. Ten to one I'd be hoarse to-morrow without this, and those blackguards would have nobody to shout at them.' He smiled down charmingly at the plump, blinking child, and she seemed struggling to say something else. But at last she said, 'Good-bye, Mister Clancy,' in her strange, unexpectedly lovely voice, and ran away, turning back once as we watched her to shout good-bye to me.

'Devil a sight of that scarf there was around when I was leaving,' Brian said, and I wondered vaguely where she'd hidden it.

'What were you going to say about writers and actors?' I said, when we were walking on again.

'I forget,' he replied. 'It must have been important.' That was typical of him; he was perpetually letting go of ideas. So unlike Diarmuid, I thought. When we were passing Tilson's there was a crowd of men gathered around a fiddler, all talking and laughing so that the strains of 'Galway Bay' had to struggle through the voices. But the magnificent head of the fiddler came up high above all the other men. He had a contemptuous smile on his lips, possibly for the tattered song that brought in the most coppers. We stopped to listen, and almost immediately the brilliant wild eyes caught us, and he bent his head graciously in greeting. When the tune had whined away to the end, the fiddler broke a path through the men with his free hand, hardly heeding the coppers that jingled into the grey tweed bag, or their donors.

'Glad I am to see you again,' the fiddler said. ' I took a great liking to the two of you.'

'You're welcome back, Mossy!' we said, and Brian jerked an eyebrow at the pub and said: 'You won't refuse a glass with us, Mossy?'

'I will not,' the fiddler said, 'only it will please me greatly.'

He had the kingly, unconscious air of conferring a favour. I was very glad we had met him. We went through a side door marked 'Lounge' in red letters, and into a square room with old panelled walls covered with photographs of horses. The chairs were hideous, tubular, chrome affairs, and the small tables had black glass tops. Michael Tilson's father, desirous of showing his prosperity, had lately disposed of all his old furniture and substituted these. Except for a shawled woman and a blue-suited man in one corner, the place was empty, though there were sounds of loud merriment from the bar next door.

'Whisky for you, Mossy?' said Brian, going over to a hatch in the far wall.

'Thank you, yes,' the fiddler said.

'You, Maeve?'

'Sherry, please. Small.' He left the order, and then came back over to the corner where we were. Mossy's eyes were moving from horse to horse along the wall. He exploded suddenly in a rich laugh, and laid down his fiddle along a side of the table.

'Those horses put me in mind of a story Mila Derrane used to tell. There was a man once filled his wall with pictures of every horse George III ever rode. Somebody said to him: "Wouldn't it be better now to have hung up pictures of all the women he kept?" "It would," says the man, "but considerations of space influenced my decision."' Mossy repeated the last sentence joyously several times.

'That lad wouldn't have been too well in with His Reverence here,' Brian said.

'No, begod,' said Mossy. 'He would not. Not that other decent men, like myself here, are either, for the matter of it. I went up last night seeing would I get a leg of a chicken by the fire—there's nowhere you would be surer of the leg of a chicken, supposing the priests were keen on giving, or supposing they took in decent normal women for housekeepers.'

'And don't they?' I said, seeing vividly the priest's housekeeper in my mind.

'They take in bitches,' Mossy said slowly. 'Bitches and daughters of bitches.'

'What did she give you?' The drinks had come, and Mossy strengthened himself before going on.

'She gave me, *a stóir*,[11] a lump of bread too hard for His Reverence, and it plastered with some class of jam. "Take it," says she, "for the love of God." "For the love of God, ma'am," says I, "I will." And I took the lump of bread and went out into the rain. There was a little slip of a girl like yourself looking at me through the window and I making down the path, and I wouldn't like to take my oath it was his niece. You can never be up to those men with white collars. She was a fine, little, clean, good-looking slip, I'll say that much for him.'

'Were you in Aherlow before that? ' Brian asked him, leaning over the glass table.

'I was,' he said, ' staying in the house of Kate Harrington, at the mouth of the glen. I came back yesterday because I couldn't remember rightly when you were acting the play.'

'By the way things are going your music will be the

---

11   *My dear.*

only thing in the play, Mossy. 'Tisn't shaping too nicely.'

'Never mind that,' the fiddler said. 'You can't build a stone house in a day. There were men outside here to-night that said the play was going to be the biggest thing in the county, and that the master had more in his head than all the other masters in Ireland together.'

'More nonsense, maybe,' the master said. And then, 'Sure, would you mind them?'

'I don't know but I would,' Mossy said, 'seeing that they are the people that will fill the schoolhouse, and you'll see, a mhic,[12] they will fill it.'

'I wonder?' Brian said, emptying his glass suddenly and then spinning it slowly through his hands on the table. It reminded me of Diarmuid spinning a cruet in Toni's, turning over a thought as the cruet moved through his pondering fingers, suddenly looking up and laughing as he planted it firmly down on the table. The long upper lip—the young, lop-sided smile.

I was aware suddenly of the fiddler's wild blue eyes staring through mine, of his head tilted towards me as if he were listening to my thoughts. Brian went over to order more drinks, and the fiddler said, so softly that I thought afterwards I'd imagined it, so intently that I can never forget the words:

'You were born solitary. Solitary as a slip of moon over the Black Cliffs. But you weren't born sorrowful, though you will bring sorrow. Forget the yellow hair. No man would ever satisfy you.' And then releasing my eyes he laughed deeply and was suddenly in the middle of a story that reached Brian over at the hatch, and the shawled woman and her man in the far corner, because they both turned listening to the fiddler, as people do around a fire.

---

12   Son.

Forget the yellow hair. Forget it? How had he known of yellow hair? Or did images leave secret traces in one's face, locked from all but the poet and the madman? Forget the yellow hair. Had I dreamed it? Yellow sun on yellow hair. It was like something I had learned by heart years ago, whose context was forgotten.

'If we go,' Brian was saying, 'we'll say you sent us. Won't we, Maeve?'

'Where?'

'Aran. We'd find stories as old as the islands there.'

'When?'

'The summer? If you don't go home.'

' If I don't go home,' I repeated, knowing suddenly that I would not go home.

'Drink it.' Brian Clancy was laughing, eyes golden, lips parted and wet with wine. He tilted part of his drink into my glass. I watched the snaky progress of the red through the clear gold. Then I drained the glass. Mossy began to play a reel, full of a wild gladness that had slept through dark centuries, but never died. The men began to come through the door from the bar, their glasses in their hands, jostling and laughing and shouting encouragement at the fiddler. Mossy played on, head tilted to the music, eyes distant, drawing from Mila Derrane's fiddle an immortal joy.

'Now, gentlemen,' Michael Tilson's father was saying, putting a worried red face around the door. 'Now, gentlemen, please! ' Nobody minded him.

II

The play was to be on Easter Saturday, and up to that morning I was irresolute whether to go home afterwards or not. I could have got a late train, which would have me in Dublin early on Easter Sunday. Even though I had decided against going home previously, I had changed my mind several times since then. There seemed to be so little point in staying at Miss Walsh's. I would agree with myself on that. But the next minute I would decide that there was still less point in going to Dublin. Faces. Sympathetic, veiled faces, evasive eyes, carefully chosen topics of conversation—a whole hideous conspiracy of studied kindness. It would be intolerable. I thought of the other faces which would somehow be less repulsive—faces of people who were simply vulgarly curious, who would question slyly as far as they dared, and use their eyes when they dared go no further. One could parry such people—but the kind ones, the sensitive people like Máire and Brendan and my mother. Growing out of the very nature of our relationship was an inalterable reticence. The very thought of her knowing everything of the whole miserable business, even expecting confidence, possibly offering consolation, made me go cold with repulsion. I couldn't face it.

Then there was the possibility of seeing Diarmuid, perhaps in some crowded place, a street or a theatre. Being forced to speak to him, coolly, like a stranger, as it would have to be.

'Hello. How are you getting on?' The forced smile. The mad racing of blood that pounded in one's ears and cut one's breath short, as after a long run.

'Fine. And you?'

'All right.' And then there would be nothing more to say, nothing more that could be said. Why doesn't he go? one would think. Intimacies that one had impudently thought eternal would have been buried for ever, buried so that nothing showed on the surface but a conventional greeting, a smile, a handshake such as one would give an acquaintance whom one would never see again. Buried for ever. It wasn't possible to face the possibility of all this, not yet. In years to come, perhaps, yes. When we were old. When the long delirium of the blood would have dimmed, and nothing remained but a faint nostalgia incapable of hurting. Then perhaps we could meet and talk intimately again of ourselves, of books, of anything.

Somewhere in the background there would be Doreen, the old, laughing, malicious Doreen with hair like water in the sun, but incapable of doing any harm ever again. The child? It would be grown up perhaps. It wouldn't be important anyhow, not then. How long would it take? Would Diarmuid's hair be yellow still, and his cheeks faintly hollowed in the tracing, and would his fingers still be softer than mine? Some time I would see a peace again in the dark mature eyes (as I had seen often when he stood on the doorstep at home) and then I would know nothing could ever intrude again. Not Doreen, not pride, not circumstances. The secret places of the soul would be mine. What did I care for the rest? But I cared now. Cared so much that the thought of the unknown delirium they had shared filled me with hatred and despair. Hatred because she had shared it, despair because I never would. No, going home wasn't possible.

And yet, at the last moment before the play began, I thought I would go. I could hear the heavy sound of the voices on the other side of the blue curtains, the scraping of the chairs, the sudden high laugh of a child. All was confusion around me—Maureen Walsh in tears, begging every girl she saw to take her part, saying she wished she were dead, clinging to Brian Clancy and imploring him to let her go home. Bridie McMahon was laughing and hugging everyone, and twirling around on one silver-slippered toe. Bassanio was gloomily combing back his oily waving hair, mumbling the speech beginning:

'So may the outward shows be least themselves.'

Everyone seemed to be on top of everyone else. There was hardly enough room to turn. A narrow passage running between a side of the stage and the wall served as a dressing-room for everyone. One small spotted mirror hung from a nail. The air was thick with smoke and perfume and cosmetics. Only Brian seemed perfectly at ease, checking coolly over all the props, Shylock's knife, his scales, the three caskets, a couple of letters, the bond, several rings. He had them all laid out on a small green card table. When they were checked he moved through us all, leaving a cool breath in his wake. He was good at smoothing people, making them see things through his happy normal eyes. He would not have known how to be nervous himself. He began to talk in a whisper to Maureen Walsh, an arm about her shoulders. She was laughing in a moment, and before he left her she was ready to walk on at once, had it been necessary. She looked impatiently at her watch, wishing the first scene away.

'Take that off,' he called to her. 'It's an anachronism.'
'It's what?'
'It's not necessary, girl. Take it off,' and she obeyed. He came over to me. 'Does the golden fleece feel all right?'
'A bit queer,' I said. 'Like a hat that's too tight. I hate hats.'
'Well, you would go having black hair.'
'The Almighty didn't consult me, Brian.'
'It's as well. You might have chosen gold. I'd rather have you black, even if we did have the expense of a wig itself. Are you all right?'
'Yes, why?'
'Going home afterwards?' His eyes were infinitely kind and friendly and golden, as they had been that evening when he had tilted up my face to a lamp, after the walk up the hill.
'No. I mean I don't know.'
'Stay. I'm not going home myself, either.'
'Why?'
'Too lazy. Too unfilial. Stay.'
'I'll tell you afterwards.'
'All right. Good luck, Maeve.'
'Thanks.' You're so normal, I thought, so normal and tranquil and healthy.

Even now, I don't remember much about the play, whether it was good or bad. I remember that I was no good myself, and that I fluffed lines four times. I remember the strained face of Brian Clancy desperately prompting in the wings, and my stupid attempt to lip-read rather than to catch his whisper. I remember all sense of the stage slipping away from me once. Are you going home? No. I don't know. Stay. Why? Afterwards.

'Then must the Jew be merciful,' I said at last, with an absurd intonation, and I was briefly aware of Brian Clancy's eyes closing in relief. And the tragedy is you'll be sorry. I'm learning. I never knew you were conceited. Shut up, I told myself desperately. Oh, shut *up*. After that I went doggedly ahead, bending my mind to the lines, and forcing them out correctly and meaninglessly, as out of a machine.

Once I was happy. Mossy was playing the tune that had been made for Cáit Óg's wedding (how long ago? Was she old now?), and the moonlight slept sweet on the bank (the trouble we'd had putting blue paper over the bulbs!), and the play was almost over. Then it was over, and there was cheering from the school benches, and Father Tom was bending and smiling and shaking hands with Brian on the edge of the stage, and saying that the town was proud of the Society now, but it would be prouder. Wild, prolonged cheering, like the cheering in Croke Park on Final day. There was no reason why this Society should not enter next season for the Kerry Drama Festival, no reason at all. Nobody in the town would grudge any help. The Children of Mary who had so kindly helped with costumes would do so again. He had no doubt of it. Neither had the town, because there was further prolonged cheering. An old gentleman with white cotton-wool hair suddenly stood up, and said it would give him great pleasure if Father Tom would accept, on behalf of the Society, a cheque for ten pounds towards the funds. He walked up to the stage to present the cheque, and it was only when I got a strong whiff of peppermint that I recognised the old gentleman who had slammed down the window that night on the train.

But at last it was all over, even the tedious little party afterwards, during which we all kept on our costumes—for the fun of it, Bridie McMahon said. It might have been fun too. But I was glad when at last they were all gone, and my golden wig was lying on a bench. The place was a desolation, but that didn't matter. The school holidays were on, and Miss Walsh, beaming with pride and good nature, had come up and whispered to Brian not to bother his head fixing anything. If he gave her the key she would tip in the next morning after Mass and leave the place like a new pin. She did, too. Her untidiness was confined to her own home.

We were glad to shut out the light on the scene of disorder and pass into the dark warmth of the April night. There was no moon and scarcely a handful of dim stars. We walked down the street, past the memorial, out towards the level-crossing. Brian made not the slightest reference to my staying, nor did I. I had made no decision really. I had simply stayed for the party, thinking every moment: 'I can still go now, if I want to, and catch that train.' But I had not gone. Now I was hardly sorry, hardly glad. I accepted the warm dark wind blowing through my hair and the forgetfulness it brought. And when the train I should have got staggered by uncertainly past our faces, pulling slackly at the hill and sending an indolent drift of sparks up into the darkness, I accepted that too. When the last carriage had swayed by, and the white gates had swung wide against the night, we went through.

'Have a cigarette,' Brian said. It was so dark I couldn't see his face until he lit a match. Thin bars of light struck through his shielding fingers and crossed his face when he bent to light my cigarette. It was the first cigarette I had ever smoked.

III

> 53 Lower Mount Street,
> Dublin,
> Wed., June 3

My dear Maeve,

The address at the top of this letter represents the outcome of winter's battle with Mother. You'd hardly have heard about it? Don't ask me what it was all about. She's an angel really, but impossible for anyone except the emotionally passive (like Daddy) to live with. That's about the only explanation there is. I'm not emotionally passive.

I hated the commercial school, and she had set her heart on my staying there until I was qualified to handle the affairs of Mr Cooney—ridiculous name! I told her after the first week that I wouldn't stick it and, of course, she refused to believe it, and was terribly sweet, buying me a new frock and bag, and offering me them the way you'd offer bullseyes to a child. I took them, of course, but they didn't make the slightest difference in my attitude to the commercial school. Learning to type nearly drove me demented, and the thought of clacking away the rest of my life for a wretched Mr Cooney! I know I said I wouldn't mind *it last summer, but I hadn't tried it then. Anyhow, I asked if I could go to college, thinking she wouldn't mind a bit. She did. She said that women with degrees were atrocities, and though there wasn't much fear of my getting one it was just possible I might. Anyhow, it would be waste of money, as I'd probably marry before I was half-way through. I pointed out that she spent more money on perfume in a year than would keep me at Oxford for three, and that I hadn't the least desire to marry in my teens and only wanted to go to UCD. She laughed at me, and bought me more lovely things, including a gold watch. She maddened me, and I told her that if she insisted on forcing me into a career I loathed, I'd leave the house. She had no idea I would, and neither had I. But out of sheer cussedness I did the W.A. exam, without telling her, and was called six weeks ago to Industry and Commerce. The first thing I did was to get this flat (a depressing little hole) and leave the house. Amusing, isn't it, Maeve?*

To tell you the truth, I only did it because I wanted to make some gesture of independence, something spectacular that would make people talk. It has. Mother's been a dear, though. She arrived here the day after I did, with the new car (forgot to tell you she would get a new car) packed to capacity with curtains and cushions and pictures and all sorts of things. Only for her the flat would be a den. There's a man with red hair directly below me, and he reads poetry all night— he must, because it's the last thing I hear before going to sleep, and the first when I waken in the morning. He's potty, I think. If he played the saxophone there'd be some sense in it. Or even the piano. But reading poetry!

I forgot to tell you he's in the office. He spends most of the day on the phone to people—unofficially, of course—and once I heard him phoning Coleridge's 'Kubla Khan.' He's in my section, and the girls here say he's leaving to join the RAF Why the RAF?

I've been meaning to write to you these ages, Maeve. When you didn't come home at Easter, I meant to then. But somehow, I kept putting it off. I'm writing now mainly to tell you some news I couldn't keep. Doreen and Diarmuid Barron were married quietly a week ago. I thought you probably wouldn't know, because people somehow always leave the telling of things like this to other people. I've known you too long to be afraid, and too well to say anything foolish like ' I'm sorry.' But I'll say this much. If Doreen expects me to be friendly, to congratulate her, and gloss over her rottenness as so many people seem to be doing, she'd better think again. You know I'm not prudish. If she had made love to a tramp and married him, I'd say good for her if that's the way she was feeling. But let her so much as smile at me ever again in the street and you'll see what will happen. You'll hear anyway.

Brendan and Máire were over in the flat last night. What a pair of innocents they are! They took me out for a drive (in our old car!) to Portmarnock, to the County Club, and when I asked Brendan if he'd wanted to put temptation out of his way, he blushed. I swear he did. And Máire's hair and face were the same colour. I suppose you're coming up for the wedding in July? You can't let them down, Maeve. They said last night they wanted you. Come, Maeve. You always said you didn't give a hoot for gossip. Prove it. And those infants will be so furious if you stay away! By the way, there's not much difference between Máire's white evening frock (remember?) and her wedding-dress—or her First Communion dress, for that matter, as Mother would say. I've seen all of them, But she's getting more incredibly beautiful every time I see her. When I think of that mouse in school!

I'm writing this in the office, under cover of a mountain of pink files. But I'd better stop now. O'Driscoll, the boss, is leaving down the phone, and he might be over. Write some time if you feel like it, and come on the 24th, won't you?

*As ever,
Nora*

So Brendan and Máire had got her to write? Still I wasn't going. Cowardice, if you like. I was going with Brian Clancy to Aran, where this whole farce would be less real to me than the sound of the sea against Dhu Caher, or the voice of an old man telling stories half as old as time. Mossy Derrane's sea-strange eyes had promised as much.

IV

Before we left for Galway in July, I had two further things I wanted to leave behind. One was George's death. Word of it had come in a brief note from Brendan. I was glad I would not have to take sherry and cake in his house, and after, go upstairs with the other people into the darkened room of death, and see the white still face and the limbs motionless on the white linen. I was glad I would not have to listen to the traditional, horrible, whispered comments of red-eyed mourners.

'Sure, isn't it well for him?'

'Isn't he better off where he is? '

'Poor George. Sure, it was only a happy release for him. A happy release, that's all it was. Ah, yes.'

'Never said a hard word to anyone.'

'One of the best.'

It was better to slip upstairs into the small sun-filled room, and look again at the only beautiful thing in it, the woodcut model of the Custom House. I touched the lovely delicate lines gently, half expecting them to crumble to a heap of sunny dust now that the maker's hands were quiet for ever. But it was no less lovely than it had been when George's great bony fingers had whittled away the last flake of wood and then touched its perfection experimentally. 'George,' I thought, looking at the satin-smooth shining dome, outlined in sun, and I thought it strange that I could think of nothing else to say to his memory. But then he had said so little to me, ever.

The second thing I wanted to leave behind me for the holiday was also a death—the death of Doreen. She had died early in July, at the premature birth of her son. I could not visualise this deathbed at all. It seemed as unreal as a badly told incident in a poor story. She was dead. I thought of the slim body arched backwards in an impromptu dance, the hair falling back from her upturned head, shining and pale as water in the sun. I thought of the sun-gold face laughing at Máire's awkwardness, of the racing figure in a brief swimsuit covering the spaces of shimmering sands with slender long legs. But of her death I could form no picture. It didn't make sense. But she was dead. I knew because I could bring up the image of her loveliness with no trace of resentment. Forever now she would be a girl racing towards a summer sea, the first to touch the first shining wave.

As we went through a July mist in the train to Limerick Junction, I believed that for two weeks at least I would be released from identity. It never occurred to me that anything from the world I knew would reach out thirty miles into the Atlantic to touch me. But it did, and in a sense, that spell in Aran was an end and a beginning. It was the end of youth and the beginning of a studied, artful indifference to pain. If I lived to be eighty (and people like I usually did) I should never again be hurt by anything. On that I was determined.

V

Galway was, as one had imagined, a city balanced perilously between two worlds. Within a stone's throw of the harbour everything—high crumbling houses, cobbled lanes and Higgins' archways of forgotten Spain—was caught into a mood of passive, pearl-grey timelessness. The misty rain was falling soundlessly from low skies, much as it had fallen four centuries ago, and it was falling on walls that were old then. Nothing had changed, not even the Spanish-dark eyes of the shawled women, glancing and passing. But outside the charmed circle of grey stone it was different. The Galway we had passed through from the Salthill Hotel where we'd stayed was vulgar, flashy, reaching out with tubular chrome fingers at the old gravity and loveliness and threatening them with strangulation. We were glad to leave the new Galway to its crowds and dance bands and tawdriness, and pass through Eyre Square down to the shrouded, cobbled harbour, that had resounded to the thump of Pádraig O'Connaire's blackthorn stick. Galway Bay was heavily veiled from the July morning. Wraith-like swans floated idly, it seemed, on the grey air. Outside a small radius of heavily moving water there was a white opaque nothingness. Somewhere out there the islands were, maybe, in an oasis of sunlight. Or maybe in rain. We waited, with a dozen or so other travellers, on the wet cobbles for the gangway to be opened. It was nine o'clock. The little steamer, *Dún Aengus*, would be sailing at nine-thirty. The mist wasn't serious—it would be blown away as easily as froth off porter in a short while. So a man in the little hut belonging to the Steamship Company had told us. I had wandered over to talk to him, tired suddenly of Brian's agreeable, happy company, wishing with a sudden stinging lust that I might have been here for the first time in Galway with Diarmuid. He might have said nothing, might merely have touched my arm to make me notice something, and yet forever afterwards the place would have been enriched, touched by a mind sensitive to the significance of every grey stone.

'Just yew look right over there, pal,' Brian Clancy said, heavily mimicking Chicago, and I followed the direction of his eyes to two long, loose-limbed American boys, with leather jackets zipped to the throat, and big hiking boots. Their only luggage was a rucksack each. 'Gee, yew did oita see the swell little islands us two bin at over in Ireland,' Brian went on. 'Kinda native and cute. Sorta places yew don't have nowhere else. Steeped in hisstory, see?'

A big powerful man, with harsh blue eyes and tight homespun breeches held up by a gay crios, motioned us over the gangway into the little steamer. We surrendered our tickets and walked up the plank on to the cluttered deck, smelling of mist and fish and ropes and dung— animals sailed constantly to and fro from the islands, down in the hold. We watched four red cows (probably bought at a Galway fair) being swung up above our heads, and lowered into the hold, eyes rolling and pitiful and terrified, tied legs feebly struggling. Afterwards, we went and looked down at them over the rails. The four of them stood close together, chin resting on the rump of the one in front. A faint steam rose upwards from their bodies. Later, penned off from them roughly we saw six pigs, equally frightened and equally still. There was no distinction on this little steamer. Beast and man were but nominally and slenderly divided. If you liked, you could go down the steps, and stroke the damp red hides, and watch the great wounded eyes staring without resentment into yours.

I went down, and Brian stood at the top of the steps and laughed: 'For God's sake, Maeve!' We were both down there when the siren went, a blurred sound in the mist, and when we went on deck the ropes were being hauled in, and a handful of people had gathered on the quay to see the last of us. There were a couple of women in black shawls carefully examining us face by face, and sometimes turning to whisper. A half-dozen or so small boys shouted and clung to the ropes, and were pushed away still shouting. Several sailors leaned against the harbour wall, smoking and watching, and a small white mongrel barked in a frenzy at someone on board. We were off then, pulling slowly out of the harbour into the mist, where already fragile limbs of sun were climbing through. By the time the emerald-and-black marbled Cliffs of Moher had risen to the left of us, the slow yellow light was flooding through a widening gap of cloud, dissolving the mist into a vague pallor at the edges of the sky. The little steamer rolled rhythmically through invisible furrows, plunging and rising, pausing, plunging again. Every whim of the Atlantic breakers registered in the movements of the *Dún Aengus*. She is a wayward, hardy, rapscallion of a steamer, giving little to the timid traveller and expecting much of him. Already a few unfortunates were lying corpse-like on the deck, covered by coats, and one shawled woman was huddled on a box near the rails where we were standing. Her whole body seemed to be gathered into the shawl, and only her dark brown face, with tightly shut wrinkled eyes, showed from a fold of it. She kept muttering like a litany (only it was all the same): 'Sacred Heart of Jesus, have mercy.'

I learned afterwards that she was not the only island woman who had been sailing to Galway regularly all her life, and yet had never failed to be seasick. The sight of people being ill on a boat had always seemed to me funny—as if they had freely and absurdly decided to be ill. There seemed to be no more reason for illness here than travelling in a bus or walking along a street. I turned to make some such remark to Brian, and found his eyes closed like the island woman's and his face a livid crumpled white, as free of colour as the churned drifts of foam below. His tanned hands gripping the rails were the only recognizable things about him, and I touched one of them, half in sympathy, half in curiosity, to see if it were cold. It was. He opened his eyes and smiled with tremendous effort. The cleft chin gave a vaguely normal and pathetic twist to his smile, and I suddenly felt like comforting him (without having the least idea how one did comfort seasick persons, or if one could). But then it struck me that actually seeing him in the act of being ill would be as unpleasant for me as it would be for him, so I squeezed the brown hand again and wandered off down the deck, perfectly and unaccountably happy.

I loved this odorous, absurd little steamer so much that I could have kissed it. I loved the throaty roar of the sea, and the rowdy cold wind that broke through my loose jacket, even through the white wool jumper, and harshly touched my skin, making it ripple and tingle.

With crepe sandals firmly gripping the boards, I raced along in a sudden ecstasy past a few recumbent figures and up towards the prow that dipped and lifted to a wild rhythm. I let myself through the low dividing gate, clicked it shut, and then in a few leaps was up at the tip of the prow, gripping the edges and standing on a coil of hard rope. My body yielded to the rhythm of the ship, plunging, climbing, poising, plunging again. Wild green waves were lurching and rioting everywhere, smashed to a million snowy fragments by this pointed prow, to the very tip of which I was clinging. It was good to be alive in this boisterous, blazing world of green waves and white foam and dizzy, spinning sunlight. It was good to be covering the heaving miles to the island—wild, dream-touched Aranmore. It was good to be feeling to the outskirts of a remote and austere western world, buoyed with the impudent hope that it would yield to oneself something never yielded to stranger before. Synge perhaps? Well, perhaps, but was there not that strange entry in the journal about his always wanting something new to amuse the people, a new tune, a card trick, more photographs? I turned my eyes to the left and saw the whale-like dark form of the small island Inisheer, and apparently beside it (but actually several miles away) the middle island Inishmaan, rising steeply into sharp black cliffs at her western tip. If this had been Wednesday, the steamer would be calling at Inishmaan with supplies; I wished it were Wednesday. Up on a headland there were a few clearly outlined figures scanning the steamer—a couple of full-skirted women, one tall man, and several children. We skirted the middle island widely and then veered left to the long jagged coastline of Inishmore. Like the other island, it rose in sharp incline to the west, and the eastern side, which we were approaching, dropped to the indigo sea in low yellow stretches of sand. It was beautiful, lying on the breast of the sea like some long, velvet-pawed monster stretched in sleep. We had skirted the little harbour of Killeaney, with its dark jutting fort inexplicably raised there by Cromwell with stones taken from the neighbouring levelled church, when I remembered the suffering Brian. I looked back along the deck, past the two American boys hanging in ecstasy over the rails (one was pointing with a pipe), past the few island women with their baskets, and there was Brian waving an arm and beckoning. I came down from the prow, pausing an instant to look down at the cattle, which were huddling miserably together, and the pigs which were lying flat in a heap, as if they were dead.

But Brian was more or less recovered, laughing and apologetic, and pale and full of excitement.

'Look!' he said, gripping my arm and pointing into the sunny, lapping waters of the harbour.

'What?' I said.

'There in front of you, Maeve. Look!' And sure enough there were dark, tumbling, joyous bodies in the water, vaulting and spinning and suddenly somersaulting into the sun, before slipping back glittering into the curve of a wave.

'The lovely things,' I said. 'What are they, Brian?'

'Dolphins,' he said, and I thought how miraculously the word described the joyful leaping bodies. Dolphins. We were now nosing straight up to the jetty in Kilronan and could see the faces of the crowds waiting for the landing. Every inch of landing-place was covered. This, we were to learn afterwards, was one of the two events of the week, both of which were 'Steamer-days.' People came walking the narrow sandy roads for seven miles, from the farthest tip of Bungowla, to see the steamer coming in, bringing the post, precious cigarettes, paraffin and other necessities that came from Galway. They were all craning above each other's heads, tall black-shawled women, many of them with infants in the crook of an arm, powerful men in blue home-spuns with rawhide pampooties on their feet and broad beautiful wool crioseanna knotted around their waists. All wore open, sleeveless, tweed vests and deep polo-necked white or navy sweaters.

There was a long line of sidecars along the harbour wall, some with drivers already mounted and flicking idle circles with their whips, some without drivers—they were probably making sure of customers by going to meet them at the gangway. Ludicrous among the islanders were a dozen or so visitors, gaily dressed summery girls in absurd high-heeled sandals and one in yellow jeans; red-faced, sun-burnt men in flannels and open shirts, several of them carrying cameras. They somehow blighted the first glimpse of Aran. Why didn't they go to Bray and stay there? This, of course, was absurd. They had as much right to break into the life of the island as we had, or as little.

Curious but friendly eyes fixed one from all sides as one came down the gangway. Visitors with cases and trunks were carefully sorted in a glance from visitors who had merely come on a day's excursion from Galway. As we came down ourselves, I was conscious of a vague disappointment, rather childish and absurd. Phrases like 'the last outpost of Gaelic civilisation,' and 'an unspoiled western world,' kept running through my mind as I looked resentfully at the high-heeled toeless sandals and the cameras. Would Aran, after all, be so different—would anywhere be different? Or was there no place left in the world where one could slip quietly into a timeless backwater, and live even for a while the untrammelled natural life?

Kilronan (I grew afterwards to love the place for its quaint, small, cosmopolitan air) proved untypical of the island. It was the only place where there were several guest houses, and two or three tiny lime-washed pubs— on the flag outside one of which Barbara Mossy Derrane used to dance. I pointed this out to Brian— McDonagh's, and he pointed to the sea wall beyond it.

'There's where the Spanish sailor got knocked into the water for himself.'

The driver turned around to look at us; we were each perched sideways on the cushioned edge of the car, and he was sitting in front. He was a broad-shouldered, unshaven, red-haired man, with bright sly blue eyes and a fighter's jawline. The eyes examined both of us carefully under the peaked tweed cap. He seemed about to say something else, but enquired:

'Tá sibh ag dul siar, an ndeadh?'[13] and we nodded. We had already told him that. He turned his head to the twisting sandy road again and flicked the red mare. She spurted briefly past the little shop that was also the post office (there were crowds of islanders standing about the door waiting for the mailbag to come up from the steamer) and then she fell easily back into the trot that was enough for any horse on this white-hot day.

'Tá sé go breagh,'[14] we shouted to the islanders, when we looked back and found them staring and smiling.

13　'You're going west, are you?'
14　'It's a fine day.'

'Tá, mhuis,'[15] they called, and we only learned afterwards that the people of Kilronan invariably talked English to visitors since it was easier than trying to follow the visitors' attempts at Irish. However, no complications were likely in the obvious remark that it was a fine day.

Ever since, I have thought of Aran always in blinding sunlight. Once Kilronan was left behind, with its few shady trees, there was nothing but wastes of glittering burning limestone as far as the eye could see to either side, and beyond that to the right stretches of violet sea reaching slumberously to the Connemara coastline and the dim sharp cones of the Twelve Pins, dream-like in the heat haze. Sometimes the solid slabs of rock were broken by green minute patches of grass, painfully 'made' (from seaweed) by the islanders. We were passing by the stone, wayside crosses erected to the memory of the dead Aran men when the driver turned to us again.

'Mossy Derrane that told ye I'd say,' he said to us in English, just as if no time had elapsed since we had spoken of Barbara and the Spanish sailor.

'Do you know him?' I parried, suddenly hoping to get this sullen man to give some opinion on the irrepressible Mossy.

'I do,' he said, turning his face to the curving road again with the air of one who has not the slightest interest in the talk.

'He's a powerful fiddler,' said Brian, closing one eye at me.

'He is,' the red driver said, not turning his face at all this time. The square wide shoulders and the fiery hair under the cap were a challenge.' And a decent, kindly

---

15   'It is, faith.'

sort of a man on top of that,' said Brian, pertinaciously.

'He is.' There was venom in the tone, a fierce implied negative, but we were strangers and any question as to the relations of one islander with his fellows was an impertinence. The face did not turn once more during the journey. But when we had looped into the high, quiet little village of Kilmurvey, and stopped outside the house—Conneely's—where we were staying, he swept us both with cool, brilliantly indifferent eyes and demanded a pound. He got it, and we learned afterwards it was twice too much.

But we didn't care. The sun was shining, the bay brimming with dark, flickering, indigo water, and from the house came the voice of a young girl singing. Three beautiful barefooted children came around a bend in the lane and stared solemnly at us, their feet dusty from the roads, the tight home-spuns reaching to below their knees. Brian asked them did they live up at the house, and they fixed him with uncomprehending, shy eyes. Then I asked them in Irish, and they answered no, and told us where they did live. Their Irish was the loveliest I had ever heard.

VI

We had been on the island a few days when Úna Cáit Mhóir took us over the rocks to Michael Derrane's house. Úna Cáit was thirteen, a coltish Spanish-dark child who was sure-footed as a goat. She worked for Conneely's and served all our meals. Her English was broken and very beautiful, but she hardly ever spoke for fear of saying something foolish. One morning she begged me in Irish to speak to her in English as often as I could, because she wanted to improve at it. When she did, she would get a great job up in Dublin. Since then, she often came out with Brian and me, showing us paths we'd never have found otherwise, and speaking now and then in her lovely blending of Irish and English. For some reason, Brian didn't like her and said she was a nuisance.

    She raced up the little sandy stretch to Michael's cottage, which was set far out on a promontory in Kilmurvey Bay. We saw her vaulting lightly over the half-door and disappearing into an intense blackness. When we got to the door it was ajar, and stepping through we found that the square flagged kitchen was almost full. The storyteller, an old man with lank white hair and the most astonishing blue eyes, was in the chimney-corner, with an ash-coloured cat curled at his feet. An old woman, with hair caught into a shining comb, faced him across the fire, and smoked a clay pipe. And all around them in a semi-circle there was a crowd gathered on stools, on a bench, on the flags. There were the two

American boys listening in tense uncomprehending silence, one with mouth half open. Beside them was a tall, straight islander whose head had a familiar angle, and just behind a blonde shawled woman leaned against him. A couple of giggling ragged children were together on the floor, and already Úna Cáit Mhóir had forgotten us. She was on the floor, arms folded around her knees, black head tilted and motionless against the old woman's white apron. I hoped she would never get that grand job in Dublin. Suddenly the eyes of the storyteller caught us, as we stood still in the doorway. He bent his head slightly and, as if it were a part of the story—for his tone never altered—he said:

'Tá fáilte róibh, a daoine uaisle.'[16]

'Bail o Dhia ar an obair,'[17] I said, remembering vaguely that this was the right thing to say on most occasions, and hoping it was right here. Almost without looking at us, the tall islander and the Americans made room on the bench, and Michael Derrane's slow rich voice went on, and his strangely youthful eyes went back to the time beyond time from which we had recalled them.

What the beginning of the story had been was easy to guess. We arrived at the point when the King of Ireland's Son was being sumptuously received at the court of the King of France. He was feasted with the newest of food and the oldest of drink. The tables were so richly loaded that they were in danger of bending to the ground. All the rarest fruits in the world were there, and all the sweetest musicians were gathered to play during the banquet. When at last it was over the King of Ireland's

---

16 *'You are welcome, noble people.'*
17 *'God Bless the work.'*

Son was led to the softest, deepest, downiest bed there was anywhere in the world, and before you could tell it he was deep in a quiet, soft, dreamless, healthful sleep, for he was tired after the heat of the bloody, fierce, gallant, audacious battle of the day. Adjective was piled on adjective, each word richer and more florid than the last, and the thin restless hands of the storyteller built the pile in air as he spoke. Such storytelling was not possible in any language less rich than Irish in synonymous words. This story probably bore the mental mark of every man who had told it in a circle of turf-light throughout the centuries. Maybe Mossy Derrane's father, old Mila, who had wanted a princess, was responsible for some of the richly wrought cadences. The storyteller's voice dropped suddenly and the thin hands hung limply. Looking up, I saw an extraordinary desolation in his eyes, a wistfulness for one knew not what. For the lost laughter and gallantry of those years? For some personal loss evoked by the story? Impossible to tell. The next moment the strife and vigour of a battle were again breaking through the toppling adjectives, and the old man's hands were moving excitedly. The King of Ireland's Son was killing all before him, striking off twenty heads with a single glittering movement of his sword. And then, amid the merrymaking of the whole country, he was wedding the Daughter of the King of France, and if they weren't happy, may we never be. And if they were, it was no more than they deserved.

With a half-weary movement he turned his head towards the flames at the end of the story, and I saw how old he was. Surely ninety, and small and fragile as if the violence of the story had drained away too much strength. The old woman with the Spanish comb jumped up amid all the exclamations of approval and began to rummage in a drawer of the dresser. She was sturdy and agile, not much over sixty, and harsh voiced. The children got up stiffly off the flags and then went scuffling into a corner. The two American boys got to their feet lazily and unwillingly, lifting lanky arms above their heads.

'Did you get all the story?' Brian asked one of them. He was a freckled, square-faced youth, with short fair hair loosely curling all over his head, and the naive, half-stupid air common to Americans.

'Not a goddam word,' he grinned; 'but it sounded swell. You?'

'Yes, most of it.'

'Oyeh? Say, could you just give us some idea—' Brian started to sketch the plot for them and they both dropped down on the bench again, devouring every word. They were interrupted by a woman, who came with an armful of knitted báinín wool caps and woven crioseanna, trying to sell them. I stepped over the feet and dropped down on the floor beside the old man, whose face was still turned almost stubbornly to the flames.

'Do you still play the fiddle, Michael Derrane?' I said to him in Irish. He faced me immediately, interest slightly softening the desolation in his eyes. I have never seen eyes at once so young and so old. He said nothing, but he smiled, and where I had expected shrunken gums I saw teeth strong and flawless, weathered to the colour of very old ivory.

'Will you play me the tune you made for Cáit Óg's wedding?' I said.

'What tune was that?' he said, and I knew he was stalling by the lambent humour playing over his face.

I hummed the tune that had delighted me on the night of the play, that had suddenly made my despair appear in a ridiculous light.

'Her daughter that's there on the bench,' the old man said. 'My granddaughter.' I looked at the blonde young woman whose light-coloured shawl had fallen back on her shoulders. Her skin was pale gold, and the features had an indolence rather strange in an Aran face. From the tune, I had imagined Cáit Óg differently—was her daughter very unlike her?

'It was Mossy Derrane that played us that tune,' I said.

'His son that's her husband,' the old man said, nodding at the giant islander so much older than the girl. The whole thing formed a fabric of dim beauty in my mind—Mossy with head tilted to his fiddle in a little room in Tipperary playing us the tune that this old man had made for Cáit Og's wedding, and somewhere miles away across a stretch of the Atlantic, Cáit Óg's daughter married to Mossy's son. There was a beauty about it I couldn't have explained, but which enveloped me when the old man reached for his fiddle and sent the little tune spinning through the kitchen.

'Will ye be going to the dance in Kilrónan on Sunday?' the old woman said in her harsh voice. She had been pressing the wool caps on the two Americans, who had been too interested in Brian's story to pay much heed.

'Is there one?' Brian said, running his hands along an exquisitely woven crios.

'There is. The whole island does be there, and Father Hynes playing for them.'

'Say, can anyone just wok in?' the curly American asked.

'With sixpence in his hand he can,' the old woman said. Her English was better than most people's—probably from selling things to visitors. She did not appear awkward and ill at ease in the strange tongue as so many did.

I noticed that the old man had turned his face to the flames again indifferently when he had finished the little tune, and when I thanked him for playing it, he didn't appear to notice. He was utterly alone at his own hearth—you could see that. He was isolated in contempt for the changed times, and in wordless regret for the years when the kitchen had heard tale swopped for tale, and his had been the best of all the good stories.

There was a dignity and a sense of tragedy about him that were impossible to forget. Perhaps he felt anger that his stories were only used as baits to lure visitors in to buy knitwear. You couldn't tell, because he was impenetrable and aloof, a shell left by the ebbing of an older and finer civilisation. I stroked the grey cat and tried to pluck up courage to tell him how much I wanted to hear more stories, that it was why I had come to Aran. But everyone was moving out and the beautiful chiselled face was averted. Brian and Úna Cáit Mhóir were calling me to come, and Brian was holding a crios in his hand.

'God be with you, Michael Derrane,' I said in Irish, and he immediately turned his face and smiled, wishing me a safe journey. I glanced back from the door into the darkened kitchen and he was again turned to the flames. The old woman was settling the things back in the drawer.

'Let you run on back and say we'll not be long,' Brian said to Una, and she raced away down the lane.

'For you,' Brian said, stopping to knot the crios

around my waist. It was too dark to see the colours in it. He drew it tighter, and caught a loop through the band, leaving two fringed edges dangling.

'Thanks, Brian. It feels beautiful, but I can't see the colours.'

'I can see the little waist still. It feels beautiful too.'

'Does it?' I loosened the fingers closing around my waist and shrugged free.

'Did you know that story before?' I said, walking on down the sandy track.

'Story? Oh yes—nearly the same one,' he sighed. 'Funny old guy. Not over friendly, I'd say.'

I said nothing. The sea sounded so close I got the impression it might leap over those sharp rocks and smother us in foam, whiter than snow in the moonless night. Why do you have to say the wrong thing, I thought, the stupid vulgar thing that breaks in splinters the heroic beauty and sorrow of the old man's mood?

'The dance in Kilronan should be fun,' he said, after a silent length of road, during which I watched, so far below, the flying fragments of spray, delicate as a white veil flung across the night. The voice was puzzled and half hurt. Prig, I said to myself. People aren't made the same, not mostly. 'There are dangers for people as alike as we are.' The shrewd, haunting voice came up suddenly to my ears after—how long? Not quite a year in time— but how long?

'It should be marvellous, Brian,' I said, gratitude to this happy uncomplicated person suddenly putting eagerness—forced, it is true—into my voice. I wanted to respond, to make up for the shadow cast by something he could never understand. I put an arm through his, though I had previously freed my arm.

'You're a funny creature, Maeve—God knows you are. You're like—like quicksilver, we'd be playing with when we were young fellows, years ago.'

'I'm sorry.'

'Sorry? For what? For being as God made you, and the sort of girl a man would follow to hell? I'm a clumsy fool—would anyone else put what I want to say that way?'

He laughed, and so did I, and we stood looking down the palely glimmering stretches of limestone to the sea, cloudy with flung spray. The sound came up to us in soft, muffled thunder, growing and dying.

'You're strange, Maeve,' he said, loosely holding me by my two hands. ' Strange and puzzling and wonderful, and I'm as common as a cabbage. But I love you. I've that much taste, and that much presumption. I love you, Maeve. Don't turn away your face. If you want it, I'll never refer to it again. I'm a fool and don't I know it? No money, and nothing even to make up to you for that—except maybe you'd count loving you so much that I have the nerve to tell you, at the risk of your never speaking to me again.' His humility, the collapse suddenly of the happy confidence I had always taken for granted, shocked me.

'Brian,' I said, looking at him, 'don't. You make me ashamed when you talk like that. If you knew how much you've helped recently.'

'But you don't love me?'

'You wouldn't want me to say otherwise. No.' The sea filled up the brief silence.

'Will you marry me, Maeve?'

'Yes.'

It was afterwards, outside Conneely's, just before we went in, that he said:

'Since you don't want it to be soon I'm content. But promise me, Maeve, you won't drive me mad by slipping through my fingers where I can't follow you. Quicksilver. Don't laugh, Maeve. 'Tis the truth. You could put up a barrier the way I wouldn't ever dare to remind you you'd promised to marry me.'

'Well, I promise.'

'If I didn't know I could make you happy, even with your not loving me, I wouldn't ask you, Maeve. But I know I could.'

'And if I didn't know it also, I wouldn't say yes. Will you trust me now?'

'With my life. And it amounts to that, anyway, girl.'

When we got in, Úna Cáit, down in the kitchen, was whistling with astonishing accuracy Michael Derrane's beautiful, tormenting, little tune for Cáit Óg's wedding.

VII

The céilí was held in the main classroom of a disused schoolhouse a short way east of Kilronan village. A few islanders stood around at the door, one of the men holding a plate, something like a collection plate in church. It was full of sixpences—the price of admission. We went into a dim little room just inside the door, where men's clothes were hanging on one side and women's on the other. A few boys and girls stood laughing together near the oil lamp. They stopped when we came in and stared in not very friendly curiosity. The hum of Irish ceased and there was silence while we hung up our things, except for the wheeze of a melodeon and the happy thump of feet in the next room. I wondered if any more visitors had come on the steamer that afternoon—I hoped not. Brian and I had been away at the tip of Bungowla and hadn't bothered coming back to see the landing. We'd been talking to a man called Pat O'Flaherty, who owned a curragh, and who had promised to take us over to the middle island for a very reasonable sum.

It was hot and noisy and very gay in the next room. A single oil lamp was suspended from the ceiling near the platform where the priest sat playing the melodeon, and the lower end of the hall was almost lost in shadows. The 'Staicín Orna' was in full swing, and the tall islanders, each wearing his cap and each with wool sweater up to his throat, swung their girls wildly from the small circle of light into the shadow, where all the couples merged in laughing, stamping confusion. A knot of Spanish sailors formed around the door, teeth brilliant in dark faces, longing eyes following the dancers. Spanish trawlers put in to Kilronan as often as in red Barbara's day, we learned afterwards, bartering cognac for eggs and potatoes and milk. They apparently never gave the priest any reason to banish them from the dances. In fact, when the 'Staicín Orna' whirled to its end, Father Hynes threw a good-natured smile towards the door and wheezed into a Strauss waltz. The Spaniards cheered briefly and one tossed a round black cap up in the air. Then they made a rush for partners, bowing to the island girls and smiling, and then swinging them into the waltz. We were looking on with interest—too much interest to dance yet—when a small fat Spaniard suddenly poured an unintelligible flood into my face, smiling widely and delightedly all the time, and the next thing I knew was dancing across the floor and being steered accurately through the maze by the beaming Spaniard. The floor was incredibly mountainous—uneven as the western coastline, and full of hollows and sudden treacherous bumps. Far down the hall in the shadows, there was a hole of about four inches in diameter, into which my foot sank, until I was lifted bodily out of it by the Spaniard, who kept shaking his head and laughing. There were three encores, and then I escaped, saying 'Gratias', and hoping it was right. I dropped on to a wooden bench at the end of the hall, and wondered how I was going to find Brian again, and if he would be annoyed. Couples were already formed for the Fairy Reel, and getting back to the door looked impossible. I started talking to an old bright-eyed islander on the bench beside me, hoping I would not have to dance again. But there were many more men than girls.

'Does Father Hynes always play at the dances?' I asked, wondering at the blue glitter of the eyes set in a face which looked really old.

'He does, young girl,' the old man said in Irish, which I had used; 'but sure 'tisn't the same as the fiddle.' And have you no fiddler on the island?' I said.

'We had three, before they all made for America. The last one went a year since July. He was a good lad for a tune, Peadar Mháire Ruaidh, but he hadn't the gift of some of the fiddlers I remember. Mila Derrane now, or his son Mossy. There were fiddlers for you.'

'I know,' I said, 'because—' I broke off because I had become aware of somebody waiting beside me, standing motionless until I should turn. When I looked up in the dim light, I looked into Diarmuid Barron's face. Even in the shadows one couldn't mistake the hair, the face.

'May I have this dance?' he said in Irish, unsmiling, still motionless. I could feel the blood draining from my limbs, leaving them light as air; a pulse hammered in my throat, cutting off breath, it seemed. I had an absurd desire to run away, to force a path through the weaving dancers and break out into the cool, starred darkness. I heard the elaborately built peace breaking in splinters around me, and had a blinding confused image of myself caught in a vortex and spinning around, around … In a moment, the thin fingers touched mine, and then I knew I wasn't staying. I broke through the swaying hot chain of bodies and through another, and another, until at last I was dodging through the Spanish sailors and out into the strong moonlight. I don't know how far I ran across the sands towards Killeaney, but I remember the breeze coming cold through a blouse, and miles away, the lighthouse on Straw Island blinking and blazing, blinking and blazing again, across the water. I raced harder when I heard feet sounding behind me, harder still until I heard a voice: 'Maeve!'

Then I stopped, drained suddenly of energy, and full of an oppressive shame at having done something melodramatic and ridiculous. I didn't raise my eyes.

'You're shivering. Here, Maeve.' He slipped his tweed jacket about my shoulders, and the warmth that flowed suddenly over me was only partly from outside. He said nothing, but began playing with the leather buttons on the jacket. Imperceptively I had slipped into another world, half forgotten, yet tauntingly familiar. A gesture would make it an inheritance for ever. A gesture would mean exile. Perplexed, I stood on the borderline, vaguely aware of soft wet sand yielding to my shoes, and the hushing voice of the sea. The moon lay still in numberless small pools left by the tide. My eyes moved from one to another. Always the same. White moon-faces motionless in water.

'It's all so pointless, Maeve.' The voice was somehow older than I remembered. But the face, when I looked up, was the same, still balanced between maturity and youth, delicate and very calm, only the straight-lipped mouth hesitant in a smile. It still had that vague radiance one could never define. As I watched, he averted his head slightly, and a shadow formed in the faint hollow of one cheek. The moon broke full on the other, showing a spangling of pale freckles. The breeze made small sounds rippling the sleeves of a white shirt. It would be so easy to slip into this world, leaving all questions and all problems behind. To smile, to touch the narrow fingers circling around a button on the jacket, and then to close one's eyes for ever on three images: a girl in a silver dress, an infant that still shouted and breathed somewhere, and a man whose happy face had been clouded when he'd said: 'Quicksilver. You could slip through my fingers where I couldn't follow you …' I had said: 'I promise.'

'Listen, Maeve. When you pull two sections of the same machine apart, both are useless. They can only function together because that's the way they were made. Look up,' and a finger lifted my chin, 'and tell me it isn't sense to fit the two parts together. A poor silly child who's paid for her folly didn't make any difference. A little schoolmaster with a Kerry brogue should make less. You know it, Maeve. So do I, and that's why, despite everything, I've followed you here, before it's too late.'

'But it is too late.' It was easy when you spoke as if repeating a lesson, almost without volition. It was easy. But you knew with a piercing clarity that you would never be young again from that moment. 'It's too late, Diarmuid. I've given a promise. And I'm not breaking it. Good-bye.'

I slipped out of the jacket and walked back quickly along the sands, and the moon hopped from pool to pool at my side. I walked more quickly, fearing footsteps. But there were none. The thump of dancing feet grew stronger, wilder, and the gaiety of a melodeon broke through into the night. It was easy.

THE END

Epilogue

By Brendan Cusack

I found my sister's manuscript one evening between *David Copperfield* and a *Collected Synge* on her shelves. Nobody else ever touches the books, or ever wants to, but whenever Máire and I visit the house I usually go up. Everybody thinks it's painful, but it's not. I like that room, once shared by Maeve and Sheila, now tidy and quiet and lifeless. Sometimes I stay there for hours reading, sitting on her bed where I sat many a time and talked to her. She and I understood each other. That is why I have risked publishing her story. Once as I sat here talking while Sheila slept, she told me that writers who say they don't write to be read are either idiots or liars. I can hear the voice, see the amused dark eyes above a white sheet. This is what she would have wanted, had she lived to want anything. But she was drowned when an Aran curragh capsized off Straw Island on a day in August. It was her second holiday there. She was twenty.

A month after we learned of her death I met Barron in Stephen's Green. I'd never liked him. Maeve's descriptions of him in her narrative are in conflict with any I could give. To me he was always a precocious and conceited schoolboy, weakly good-looking, with hands that seemed to have been made for pawing women. My first impulse was to pass him by as he stood on the bridge staring down into the lake, his shoulders hunched. I can't think what second impulse made me touch his elbow and say:

'Hello, Barron, how are things?'

He looked up calmly, no glimmer of recognition on the pale, weak face. He stared unblinking and unsmiling for several seconds, like a stupid pupil pondering the answer to a simple question. I wished I hadn't stopped. But the September afternoon was thick with heat, and even in the Green the trees seemed not to shadow, but to radiate hotter currents of air, which made me decide that since I had stopped the fellow it would be simpler to go into the cool of a pub.

'Will you nip over to Fleming's with me?' I said. He nodded, and we went across, cutting through a street of Georgian houses.

'When are you taking your second Arts, Barron?' I asked him, when the drinks were before us. He raised the womanish, absurdly delicate hand and half-emptied his whisky before replying.

'I'm not,' he said.

'Why?'

'I've given up.' There was extraordinary weakness in his face, added to a touch of the conceit Maeve had always denied. As I'd expected he offered no further explanation, and I would not flatter him by questioning. We talked of neutral matters for a while, and then I said I had better be getting back to the office. Out of courtesy, since he was alone, I asked him if he'd like to walk down that far with me, and he shook his head.

'I've to catch the Galway train this evening.'

'Holidays?' I said.

'Yes,' he said carelessly, 'long holidays. I'm going over to the Aran Islands for a spell.'

'To Aran?' I was incredulous and suffocated by sudden anger that I couldn't have precisely explained. I had never been there, and never would be now.

'I'd planned to go before.' His eyes closed and were puzzled when he raised them again. 'Months ago I thought of going there. And I am going.'

It would have given me pleasure to feel my knuckles crunching into the bones of the uplifted, weak chin. I did nothing so absurd. I left him huddled in the corner there, refusing the drink he offered.

As I walked down Molesworth Street I wondered why a mere boy ten years younger should arouse such antipathy. Then I remembered an expression on Maeve's face in an unfinished house one day in spring, and I understood.

Later that afternoon, after five, when myself and Byrne and another IO went back to Fleming's for a pint, Barron was still there exactly as I had left him, heedless as a stone or a tree. He swallowed three whiskies absently while we were there, and I made no attempt to catch his attention. In any case it would have been difficult. He just sat hunched there like a man concentrating hard on a passage in a book, only he had no book. We left him there after us.

June 1948
March 1949

About the Author

Val Mulkerns was an Irish writer and member of Aosdána. Her first novel, *A Time Outworn*, was released to critical acclaim in Ireland in 1951. She was associate editor and theatre critic for *The Bell* and later worked as a journalist and columnist and was often heard on the radio. She is the author of four novels, three collections of short stories, two children's books and many published essays and critical writings. *Antiquities*, her linked short story sequence, was a joint winner in 1984 of the AIB prize for literature. In 1953 she married Maurice Kennedy and they have two sons and a daughter.

A third edition of her 1984 novel, *The Summerhouse*, was published in 2013, followed by a volume of her collected short stories, *Memory and Desire* in 2016. Her tenth title, the memoir *Friends With The Enemy*, came out a year later. She passed away in March, 2018. This special edition of her first book is published on the anniversary of her birth on 14 February, 1925.

For more information please see:

www.valmulkerns.com

451
Editions
www.451Editions.com